TRULY WILDLY DEEPLY

Also by JENNY McLACHLAN

FLIRTY DANCING
LOVE BOMB
SUNKISSED
STAR STRUCK
STARGAZING FOR BEGINNERS

ABOUT THE AUTHOR

Before Jenny started writing books about the Ladybirds (Bea, Betty, Kat and Pearl), she was an English teacher at a large secondary school. Although she loved teaching funny teenagers (and stealing the things they said and putting them in her books), she now gets to write about them full-time. When Jenny isn't thinking about stories, writing stories or eating cake, she enjoys jiving and running around the South Downs. Jenny lives by the seaside with her husband and two small but fierce girls.

Twitter: @JennyMcLachlan1

Instagram: jennymclachlan_writer

www.jennymclachlan.com

TRULY WILDLY DEEPLY

JENNY McLACHLAN

BLOOMSBURY
LONDON OXFORD NEW DELHI NEW YORK SYDNEY

Bloomsbury Publishing, London, Oxford, New York, New Delhi and Sydney

First published in Great Britain in March 2018 by Bloomsbury Publishing Plc
50 Bedford Square, London WC1B 3DP

www.bloomsbury.com

BLOOMSBURY is a registered trademark of Bloomsbury Publishing Plc

Copyright © Jenny McLachlan 2018

The moral rights of the author have been asserted

A CIP catalogue record for this book is available from the British Library

ISBN 978 1 4088 7974 0

MIX
Paper from
responsible sources
FSC® C020471

Typeset by RefineCatch Limited, Bungay, Suffolk
Printed and bound in Great Britain by CPI Group (UK) Ltd, Croydon CR0 4YY

1 3 5 7 9 10 8 6 4 2

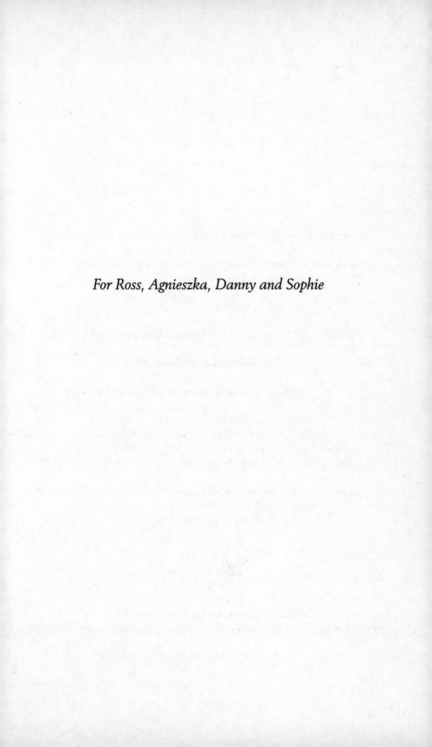

For Ross, Agnieszka, Danny and Sophie

ONE

I am sitting on a train waiting for my adult life to begin. If my mum wasn't standing on the platform watching me this would be a really kick-ass moment.

'Go away,' I mouth through the glass, but she just smiles, sips at her frappuccino and stays exactly where she is. So I stick my tongue out at her and she sticks her middle finger back at me. For an infant-school teacher, she can be very rude.

'Annie!'

I look up to see Jackson Wood, a boy from my old school, walking towards me. He's got a skateboard tucked under his arm and everything about him is relaxed and floppy: his walk, his hair and definitely his jeans.

He drops into the seat opposite me, spreads his arms wide and grins, as though his presence is the greatest gift I could receive.

1

'What are you doing here?' I say, laughing.

'Same as you. Starting Cliffe College.'

'But I thought you were staying on at school?'

He shrugs. 'I was, until yesterday, when I finally looked through that stuff they sent us and found out we had to wear *business dress*.' He says these last two words with a tone of utter disgust. 'So I rang Cliffe and they said I could enrol today.'

'Jackson, let me get this straight: you've decided to go to a college that's twenty miles away from where you live just so you can wear denim?'

He nods earnestly. 'And trainers.'

'Wow …' I say.

He smiles and relaxes back in his seat. 'Guess what I did this summer, Annie.'

'Read all of Dickens's novels?'

'Not quite. I learnt to put my fist in my mouth. Do you want to see?'

I glance around the carriage. It's packed full of commuters and teenagers – teenagers who might also be starting at Cliffe College and so could become my future friends.

'Yes,' I tell Jackson. 'I do want to see that.' If any of these teenagers are going to Cliffe, they might as well know what I'm like right from the start.

2

I watch in fascinated horror as Jackson pulls at his lips and slowly, slowly crams his fist into his mouth. Jackson has this beautiful, sophisticated girlfriend called Amelia and it's at moments like this that the whole Amelia–Jackson thing baffles me. Amelia plays the electric harp and got into the semi-finals of the Junior Fencing Championships; Jackson puts his fist in his mouth ... *What* do they talk about? Perhaps their souls meet on some amazing cosmic level that I'm too cynical to understand ... Looking at Jackson, the majority of his fingers now squished into his mouth, I find that hard to believe.

'Ta-da!' Jackson mumbles, and I give him a round of applause for effort. He wipes his slimy fist on his jeans then leans towards me and lowers his voice. 'Annie, don't freak out, but there's a woman standing on the platform staring right at you.'

'I know. It's my mum. Ignore her.'

'It's hard. She's standing so close to the window.' Jackson turns and gives Mum a wave and she waves back. Mum was supposed to just drop me outside the station, but then she insisted on coming right on to the platform. Amazingly, even though I'm sixteen this is the first time I've ever been on a train on my own.

I'm lucky my dad lives in Greece, or he'd be standing on the platform next to her. Dad can be a little overprotective and he doesn't really want me to go to Cliffe College. This morning, he put all his anxiety into one text: Annie, I hope today brings you many riches! I also hope you have a coat as there is a 50% chance of precipitation. DO NOT leave your drinks unattended, even for a moment. Boys are wicked. And wear appropriate clothes. Daddy xxx

I replied: Clothes?! I didn't realise I had to wear clothes …

Jackson sits back in his seat, leans forward again, then wriggles around, like he can't get comfy.

'Stop it,' I say. 'You look like you need a wee.'

He runs his hands through his hair, messing it up. 'Well, I don't. I'm just nervous. New college, new friends. I've only had a day to get used to the idea and it's making me feel sick.'

I know what he means. I've had all summer to get used to the idea of going to Cliffe, but I still couldn't eat any breakfast this morning. 'Listen, Jackson,' I say. 'All the best, *coolest* things in life begin with nausea: bungee jumping, freediving, kayaking down rapids –'

His eyes light up. 'You're right! Wrestling crocodiles, going over waterfalls in a barrel –'

'No, Jackson, those things aren't cool. They're ways of dying.'

But he's not listening. Instead, he's running through some bucket list of death he's got. 'Riding an angry bull, jumping off a cliff in a wingsuit, zorbing a wave, cuddling a tiger …' He breaks off. 'This isn't helping, Annie. It's making me feel worse.'

'What you need, Jackson, is a Tic Tac.' I find the little box in my bag and shake a couple of mints into his hand.

'Why do I need these?'

'Because these are *magic* Tic Tacs.' I pop one in my mouth. 'They make you invincible so you don't need to worry about anything.' That's almost word for word what Mum told me this morning when she dropped them in my rucksack. She's been telling me that foodstuffs are magical for years – super-strength Snickers, mega maths Maltesers. She should have stopped doing it a long time ago, but it makes her happy so I don't complain.

Jackson sits back and sucks. 'We're definitely doing the right thing,' he says, mainly to reassure himself. 'I mean, look at us: we're going on an adventure.'

An adventure … A ripple of excitement runs through me. 'You're right.' I say. 'The journey's only half an hour, but this definitely feels good. It feels …' I pause as I try to find the right words, 'like the *start* of something.'

'Put it here, partner,' he says, raising one hand in the air for a high five.

5

'No way,' I say. 'Not doing that.'

Suddenly, the train lurches forward and my eyes shoot to the window. Mum starts trotting alongside the train, blowing kisses with both hands. Jackson pretends to catch the kisses then stuffs them in his mouth.

'Stop eating my mum's kisses!' I say, thumping his arm.

Then the train picks up speed and when I turn to look out of the window again, Mum has gone. I didn't even get to wave goodbye.

My stomach lurches. I'm all on my own. Jackson doesn't count.

The train snakes out of town, past rows of houses with net curtains and rectangular gardens. I stare through the window and see washing drooping on lines, a broken goalpost, a man smoking in his T-shirt and pants. The man raises a mug to his lips, but before he's taken a sip, we've left him behind and the train is crossing the marsh. Then we're sliding past green fields, rolling hills and munching cows. One of the cows lifts up her heavy head and looks right at me.

Just then, the sun breaks through a cloud and shines on my face, and the train sways from side to side. *That's right, cow. Check me out. I'm on a train, on my own, going on an adventure!*

Then happiness washes over me, pushing away any worries I have and filling me up from the top of my curly hair to the tips of my Nikes.

I see this little kid peering between the seats at us. He's not staring at my wheelchair – although it is an eye-catching lime green – he's staring at Jackson, who is now trying to fit a whole apple in his mouth.

'Go on then,' I say, lifting up my hand. 'Put it here.' Jackson gives up on the apple and we slap hands. 'But we're *not* doing this on a daily basis.'

TWO

For me, it was an obvious choice, leaving my old school and going to Cliffe.

My teachers and the students were nice enough – some were amazing – but I wanted a fresh start. At school you get assigned a role on day one – the brainy one, the pretty one, the one who turned up with his leg in a plaster cast because he fell down a badger hole (Jackson) – and that's it, you're stuck with it.

For fair enough reasons, I was assigned the role of Mouthy Girl With Cerebral Palsy and I enthusiastically fulfilled this role for five years. But when my Learning Support Assistant, Jan, told me that she was going to carry on being my LSA in the Sixth Form, I realised I needed a change. Jan's lovely – she used to give me a home-made flapjack every Friday – but I knew it was time for me to go out into the world alone. No Mum, no Jan. No support. No assistance. Just Annie.

Jan got it. In fact, she suggested Cliffe. Mum put up a bit of a fight, pointing out how much she'd have to pay on train fares, but I reminded her that Dad would contribute. He only sees me a few times a year so experiences a lot of guilt. Guilt that can be eased by sending cash my way. I try not to exploit this vulnerability of Dad's ... but I do own thirteen pairs of trainers.

And that's why, right now, I'm flying through the countryside, wearing cut-off dungarees instead of sitting in assembly wearing business dress.

'There it is,' says Jackson, pointing out of the window.

Cliffe College is spread out on the edge of the town, all modern buildings with lots of glass. As the train slows, people start to get their stuff together, and then, with a final hiss of the brakes, the train comes to a stop.

Jackson jumps to his feet and follows me as I swing my wheelchair round. The doors slide open and as arranged there's the porter, slamming the ramp into place and checking it's secure. Behind me, I feel the prickly impatience of the other passengers waiting to get off. I don't care. They can shuffle and check their phones all they like: this is a rare occasion where I get to go first.

'The funny thing is,' Jackson says in a loud voice, 'she can walk. I've seen her!'

I make a grab for him, but he dodges round me and jumps off the train.

Outside the station, Jackson darts towards Tesco Express. 'Back in a minute,' he says. 'Do you want anything?'

'Yeah, a Twix would be good.' Now I've survived the train journey, I'm regretting skipping breakfast.

'I'll catch you up,' he says, leaving me to go up the hill towards Cliffe.

This hill is one of the reasons I'm using my wheelchair today. Jackson's right – I can walk – and I was fine on the train, but the five-minute walk from the station to college would have been hard work. I don't want to turn up exhausted on my first day.

Soon I'm in the middle of a stream of people all moving in the same direction. I could go faster, but I hang back so I can take everything in, or, more precisely, so I can indulge in one of my favourite hobbies: people watching.

I notice how much thought everyone's put into their appearance, especially the people who want to make it look like they've put in no thought at all. Take the girl walking in front of me. Her hair is plaited, but just the right amount of strands have been pulled loose and I can see that the price label is still stuck to the bottom of her undone trainers. A random collection of charity bracelets, leather thongs and beads rise up her left wrist, but they've been arranged by colour. There's nothing random about them, or her, at all.

I've put a lot of thought into what I'm wearing today because: a) I love fashion; and b) if people are going to stare at me, then I might as well give them something awesome to stare at. I've made my hair big and curly – kind of a Greek Afro – and I'm wearing a varsity cardigan, buttoned shirt, cut-off dungarees and my gold letter 'I' necklace. I'd describe my look as Sporty Vintage High School Greek Geek … With A Touch Of Bling. Mum described it as 'a bit odd', but what does she know?

Jackson catches up with me just as I'm going into college.

'Here you are,' he says, handing me my Twix.

I tear it open, then Jackson and I watch as people swirl round us – the older students shouting out to each other; the new students eyeing each other cautiously. Suddenly, a salty smell hits me and I notice that Jackson's holding a greasy bag.

'Jackson, what *is* that?'

'A roast chicken.'

I shake my head and put down my Twix. The meaty smell is hard for a vegetarian to take first thing in the morning. 'You are so very surprising, Jackson.'

'Thanks,' he says, with a nod and a smile. 'Right, I'm going to find my form room. Wish me luck.'

'You don't need it. You've had two magic Tic Tacs.'

'Oh yeah!' he says, then he disappears up a flight of stairs, giving me a final wave.

I turn and head towards my own form room. I know the way because I had an orientation day during the holidays. I stop outside S12, pouf up my hair, check the corners of my mouth for caramel, then pop another Tic Tac – I need a lot of invincibility to see me through the next few minutes.

I take a deep breath and push open the door.

A group of teenagers turn to look at me and I look back at them. I know it's wrong to judge people on first impressions, but I'm fairly certain it's what they're doing with me so I allow myself to indulge, just for a moment.

I see three big sporty boys looking uncomfortable in their plastic chairs; one boy sitting on his own with his hands clutching a briefcase; four girls with perfect everything – hair, make-up and clothes; a girl with cornrows and massive yellow specs; two clever-looking

12

boys; and a couple of smiley girls, the kind that get asked to babysit.

An awkward silence fills the room. I'm fairly certain it was like this before I came in, but I still feel a certain responsibility to break it.

'Hi. I'm Annie,' I say.

I get thirteen smiles and nods back, but the specs girl gives me a big grin.

With all their eyes on me, I move my wheelchair over to the wall and put on the brakes. Then I tighten the straps on my rucksack, put my feet on the floor and grip the push rings. You know when you go swimming, and you can either jump straight in or inch slowly deeper and deeper into the water? Well, I'm a jump-right-in kind of person. I push myself up and out of the wheelchair, then I walk across the room.

Well, I say I *walk* …

My knees and toes point inwards, towards each other, and with each step I take my hips jerk from side to side. So I don't lose my balance, my arms swing about too … oh, and my butt sticks out. It's my walk, but it's not most people's walk, which is why thirteen pairs of eyes are watching every step I take. I look up and meet their gaze. Thirteen pairs of eyes flick away.

'I've got mild cerebral palsy,' I say, 'spastic diplegia.'

13

Cautiously, the thirteen pairs of eyes rise again as I take a seat next to the specs girl.

I take a sip of water and another Tic Tac – projecting immense confidence is tiring – then, when I'm ready, I look up.

'Hi,' I say, smiling.

She grins back at me. She has big eyes and beautifully round cheeks that for some reason remind me of apples.

'I like your dungarees,' she says in a rush. She's got this throaty voice that doesn't match how sweet she looks. 'I've got a pair like them, but in blue.'

'Thanks,' I say. 'I love them, but they're annoying when you go to the toilet.'

'Totally! I keep dropping the straps in wee.'

I like this girl. She says whatever pops into her head.

She pushes up her specs. 'My name's Hilary.'

'Hi,' I say. 'I like your glasses.'

'I know, yellow frames – how cool? I got them in a charity shop in Devon.'

While Hilary and I discuss the pros and cons of dungarees, yellow and charity shops, everyone around us starts chatting too. I love moments like this. The start of things. The smiley girls swap numbers, the clever boys have an earnest chat and the perfect-looking girls talk to

14

the sporty boys. I glance across the room and notice that the only person not joining in on this high-speed bonding exercise is briefcase boy. My heart goes out to him, but I don't go over because Hilary has just claimed that I once tied her to a chair and this I need to follow up.

'I did *what?*'

She does her gravelly chuckle. 'It was at playgroup. You tied me to a chair in the Wendy house and I missed the apple and toast.'

'Apple and toast … that rings a bell.' I have no memory of Hilary, but Mum's told me I did some crazy stuff at playgroup so she could be telling the truth. 'Sorry about that,' I say.

'That's OK. I enjoyed it.'

Interesting …

Hilary's eyes light up. 'I thought you were amazing because you wore boys' clothes and had all these T-shirts with dinosaurs on them.'

Yep. She definitely knows me.

'Was there anything else I did? Only, we should probably get it all out in the open right now.'

'Well, you taught me the words "willy" and "guff" and you told me that one of the helpers would be pleased if I painted her handbag with Tippex.'

'I'm guessing the helper wasn't pleased?'

'No. Oh, and once you made me do a wee in the sandpit.'

Oh, God. 'How did I *make* you do that?'

'You said you'd make me eat it if I didn't.'

'The wee or the sand?'

'The sand.'

'Wow,' I say. 'I was a psychopath … Can I just apologise all in one go for everything my four-year-old self did?'

'You don't need to.' She hits me with her massive smile. 'You were so funny!'

I'm saved from hearing any more revelations by our new form tutor walking in. Mr Cobb apologises for being late, sloshes coffee over his desk and then hands round soggy timetables. I see that my first lesson today is English literature.

Hilary leans towards me and whispers, 'Do you remember when you told me we were only allowed to use the trampoline if we took off *all* our clothes?'

THREE

One of the perfect girls, Romilly, has the same first lesson as me so I leave my wheelchair in S12 and we walk there together. I've got a pair of crutches stored in Mr Cobb's cupboard – Mum dropped them off last week – but I decide to see how I'll get on without them. With difficulty, it turns out. The corridors are packed and I have to concentrate hard on keeping a conversation going, getting up a flight of stairs and not falling over. Falling over is one of the more out-there side effects of my cerebral palsy.

By the time we reach the classroom, I'm hot and my heart is racing. Thank God for Mitchum Ultimate. Seriously, the stuff's amazing.

While Romilly goes to sit with a couple of friends, I go to an empty desk by an open window. I take another sip of water and let the cool air from the window wash over me. I could have sat with Romilly, but I prefer sitting on my own – I like to spread out – plus I don't want to get sucked into a gang of girls on my first day and then have to hang out with them for the next two years.

Our teacher, Miss Caudle, is a young, slim woman with flame-red hair. She takes the register then hands round copies of the book we're studying, *Wuthering Heights* by Emily Brontë. I pick up my copy, hold it close to my nose, then flip through the pages and breathe in deeply.

'Ah, a fellow book sniffer,' says Miss Caudle.

I nod and take another sniff. 'New book is my favourite smell in the world.'

'Well, that's your new book now so write anything you want in it.' She turns to the rest of the class. 'That goes for all of you: record your thoughts inside your books. *Wuthering Heights* is arguably the most powerful love story ever written and I want to hear your opinions about it.'

I take in the mist-shrouded couple on the front cover and have to stop myself from rolling my eyes – I'm not into romances – but then Miss Caudle starts describing the 'terrible violence and cruelty in the novel' and I perk up.

We're just going through the characters when the classroom door swings open and an exceptionally tall boy with short blond hair strolls in. He's wearing jeans, a tight zipped-up tracksuit top and black trainers. Curiously, draped round his neck is a fringed scarf. He looks like a gymnast who's had a rummage through his mum's accessory drawer. He walks straight up to our teacher and clasps her hand.

'Miss Caudle,' he says, although he has a strong accent and it actually comes out as 'Miss Cuddle'. 'I'm sorry I am late, but an error on my timetable sent me to the wrong room.'

'Ah ...' Miss Caudle stares wide-eyed at her hand that's being pumped up and down. 'Are you Fabian Kaczka?'

'Yes, that's me. Fabian Kaczka.' He says his surname much more smoothly than Miss Caudle, with a long 'sh' sound in the middle. '"Kaczka" means "duck",' he adds, then he quacks. Loudly. In Miss Caudle's face.

Across the classroom, people gasp and stifle giggles.

Fabian Kaczka turns to face us, points at us and says, 'But you guys call me Fab.'

A boy at the front bursts out laughing, then says, 'All right, *Fab*.'

Fab, either not caring or oblivious to the fact that this boy is laughing at him, sticks out his hand and says, 'You've got it, my friend. Put it here.'

The boy watches in horror as Fab involves him in a blokey hand grab.

Quickly, as if she fears Fab might shake hands with everyone in the class, Miss Caudle tells Fab, 'Take a seat. Anywhere you like.'

His eyes sweep across the classroom, studying everyone in turn, before finally falling on me.

Ah, come on. Move on, eyes, I think. I'm enjoying sitting all on my own at the back, watching everything that's going on. But Fab's clearly made up his mind because he gives a determined nod then walks straight towards me, past several empty seats.

He stops in front of my desk, does this little bow and says, 'Please may I sit with you?'

Well, this is awkward.

As everyone watches to see what I will do, I feel my cheeks go red. I've just done my special walk across college, totally blush free, then Fab Kaczka bows at me and I go red!

'Sure,' I say, with a nonchalant shrug, then I take another drink of water to suggest my redness is solely down to dehydration and I move my stuff across.

Fab unwinds his scarf, places it carefully over the back of his chair, then sits down. He's so tall that I have to shift towards the window to stop our shoulders from touching. Next, he takes a fountain pen, a yellow notebook and a pad of paper out of his bag, then turns to look at me.

Woah. Those are *blue* eyes. They are the *exact* shade of Mum's Bombay Sapphire gin.

'Hello,' he says.

'Hi.' I pointedly keep my hands on my book. There will be *no* handshaking going on here. This boy clearly doesn't understand boundaries and I don't want to encourage him.

After looking at me for a moment longer, Fab turns to the front of the class, rests his chin in his hand and shifts his intense attention back to Miss Caudle – or, should I say, Miss *Cuddle*.

Finally, the lesson can begin.

FOUR

I love reading. I mean, I'm obsessed with it. I'm a book pervert, and I do it everywhere and at every opportunity, even when I probably shouldn't be doing it at all: during assembly, when I'm talking to my Greek nan on the phone (or rather when she's talking to me), when I get bored during films. Some people think that when you read you're shutting yourself off from the world. But they're wrong. When I read, my world just gets bigger and better.

Occasionally, back at secondary school, I'd get a sympathetic look from a girl in my year – *Bless, Annie's READING again, like someone from the olden days!* But I didn't care because generally I was reading a high-octane, violent thriller that I knew had to be better than whatever she was doing (usually her hair). Plus, the difference between what you can get away with reading about in public and *looking at* in public is mind-boggling.

So, I'm pretty much in heaven as Miss Caudle, eyes glittering, carries on describing the various characters in *Wuthering Heights*. She shows us pictures of the Yorkshire moors where Emily Brontë lived, and of the waterfalls and crags that appear in the book. As she talks, I type.

Next to me, Fab writes an endless stream of notes in large, flowing handwriting. I don't recognise the language he's writing in, but I see that it's bouncy, with lots of curly 'K's and 'J's.

Soon Miss Caudle tells us to read the opening chapter and make notes of our first impressions.

With a tingly sense of anticipation, I open the book and start to read. On the surface, nothing particularly dramatic happens – a man called Lockwood goes to this isolated, sinister house to pay a visit to his grumpy landlord, Heathcliff – but every word is loaded with menace and I get the feeling something very bad is about to happen.

It's a good feeling, which is why it's annoying when Fab leans towards me and says, 'Excuse me.'

I put my finger on the book, then look up. 'Yes?'

'What is your name?'

'Annie.'

He nods. 'So, *Annie*, I have a quick question: what is a "misanthropist"?'

'A person who dislikes human beings.' *Like me right now*, I think.

'Thank you.' Fab writes something in his yellow notebook.

I turn back to a description of Heathcliff as a 'dark-skinned gypsy' and 'gentleman'. I draw a line under the words and write *race and class?* in the margin.

Two minutes later, I get another 'Excuse me', followed by: 'Annie, what is "peevish"?'

'When you feel irritable.' *Like me. Right now.*

Ten seconds later: 'Annie, what is "penetralium"?'

'I don't know.' I hold up *Wuthering Heights*. 'This was written over a hundred and fifty years ago – it's full of archaic words.'

His eyes widen. '*Archaic?* What is "archaic"?'

'Words that aren't used much any more, but –'

Fab shushes me as he jots something down. 'Annie, it is very important that I learn the meaning of every word.'

'OK, but I don't know the meaning of all the words.'

A cough from the front of the room makes us look up. 'If you two could keep it down,' says Miss Caudle, 'just so everyone can concentrate on the task.'

Great. Now Fab's got me into trouble. Me getting into

trouble was another thing I wanted to leave behind when I came to Cliffe. I wasn't out of control at school, but I did get *a lot* of detentions. I blame this on my fiery Mediterranean temperament, but Mum's less generous and says that sometimes I can be a right pain in the ass. Whatever the reason, I don't want to draw attention to myself on my first day.

'Sorry,' I say to Miss Caudle. Then I whisper to Fab, 'You need a dictionary.'

'Like this?' He pulls a red book out of his massive rucksack. It says *POLSKO–ANGIELSKI* on the front. So he's Polish.

'Wouldn't it be easier to use your phone?'

He dismisses my words with a shake of his head. 'No. I prefer this.'

'But wouldn't your phone be more practical?'

'More practical, yes, but less reliable.'

'Well, OK,' I say with a smile, then I turn back to *Wuthering Heights*, leaving Fabian Kaczka tutting, drumming his fingers and flicking through his massive dictionary.

For the rest of the lesson, he keeps relatively quiet, but when Miss Caudle tells us to pack up, he unleashes a torrent of questions. 'Annie, why were you using different coloured highlighters in your book?'

'I'm using a different colour for each theme. It's something my teacher in my old school taught me to do.'

He nods then says, 'Why do you have the letter "I" on your necklace when your name is Annie?'

I'm a bit taken aback by this – my necklace is tiny, a gold 'I' on a thin chain, too small for anyone to notice. 'My mum got it for me for Christmas.' Automatically my fingers touch it. 'She ordered it online, but they sent the wrong letter. We only found out when I opened it on Christmas Day. I told her I liked the "I" and wanted to keep it.'

All the time I've been talking, Fab has been putting things in his bag and listening intently. He starts to wind his scarf back round his neck. 'And *Wuthering Heights*? Do you like that too?'

'Yes, so far I love it. It's very dark.' I shut my laptop and start gathering up my things. Break's going to be over if I don't hurry up.

'Dark? In what way?'

I turn to look at him. He's standing there, patiently waiting for my answer.

'I like the way everything feels claustrophobic and also the words that have been used: *devil, fiend, possessed swine*.'

He nods. 'Yes, words are very powerful.'

26

I'm not used to boys saying this kind of thing. Or girls. I'm used to them saying things like 'Shakespeare's boring' and 'God, I hate poetry'.

I nod. 'Yes, they are.'

The classroom's almost empty, but Fab is still hovering by our desk. 'It's breaktime,' he says. 'Let's go to the canteen and talk about books. I will buy you a coffee. Or tea. Do you prefer tea?'

I laugh and shake my head. 'You go ahead. I want to get organised.'

'No. It's fine. I can wait.'

I shrug, then I deliberately take my time checking my phone, slipping it in my pocket, pushing my chair back. I guess I'm hoping Fab will give up and go, but he just stands there, arms folded, like he's got all the time in the world. Having him hovering next to me makes me feel like I've got my old teaching assistant, Jan, back.

Fab's eyes follow me as I tighten my rucksack straps and a familiar flutter of irritation rises inside me, just like it used to at school when I'd have to convince Jan that, no, I really didn't want her to wait outside the toilets for me, and, yes, I really would be fine in DT without her.

I must be frowning, because Fab says in a concerned voice, making him seem even more Jan-like, 'What is the matter, Annie?'

27

'Nothing,' I say, standing up.

He steps aside and I walk past him towards the door, and, just as I expected, he watches me closely. I mean, he was curious about my laptop so my walk must be absolutely fascinating for him. Suddenly, he rushes ahead, pushes the door and holds it wide open for me.

I look from the door to Fab, then say, 'Why are you doing that?'

He shrugs. 'To help. You're an invalid.'

I blink and stare at him. My heart instantly speeds up. All morning I've felt so strong, almost invincible, but with one word, Fab Kaczka has whisked my confidence away from me.

And this bothers me more than what he actually said. I thought I was stronger than that. I thought I was over being hurt by words.

Suddenly I feel mad – with Fab, and with myself.

I take a step towards him. 'A piece of advice, Fab: probably best to avoid that word. It's a bit offensive.' I see Miss Caudle look up from her desk. My voice is raised, but I don't care. 'It suggests worthlessness. *In*-valid. Like you said, words are powerful.' I take the door from him and step through it. I wiggle it backwards and forwards. 'And look: I can open doors all by myself!'

I'm halfway down the corridor when I wonder if I was

28

too hard on Fab. It's hardly his fault if he hasn't fully grasped the complex nature of the English language yet. And all that door wiggling I did … For a moment, I consider waiting for him to catch up so that I can explain that personally I think 'disabled' is a better word to use than 'invalid' and take him through the numerous ways that language can cause offence.

No. I've already missed five minutes of break because of Fab and I'm hungry.

I push him to the back of my mind and head for the coffee shop, taking the stairs instead of the lift and saying a cheery 'Hi there!' to a girl whose eyes are glued to my bare, wobbling legs.

FIVE

At the coffee shop, I get my travel mug filled with tea, choose a waffle then look across the common room. It's rammed and noisy – every seat is taken. R & B is blaring out of the speakers and there's a lot of Big Laughing going on – heads thrown back, cackles, the type of laughter that seems designed to make you feel left out.

Over in the corner, I see Hilary, sucking on an apple juice carton. I walk towards her, deliberately going through the middle of the room, and the stares I get make me feel better, because I meet them head-on.

When I get to Hilary, I'm back in control. I'm at Cliffe, where I chose to be, and I'm not going to waste a moment feeling insecure.

'Hi,' she says, shuffling over so I can share her seat. 'I feel totally lonely. There must be over a hundred people in here, but I hardly know anyone, and the ones I *do* know I don't want to talk to.'

'I know what you mean,' I say, as Georgina Carr, a grade-A bitch from my old school, walks past. Her eyes settle on me, then they flick away. 'But think of it as an opportunity. In this room, there are over a hundred people who may be lucky enough to hang out with us.'

'OK,' she says, nodding and sipping her juice.

I finish my waffle in two bites. 'Right,' I say, dropping my paper plate in the recycling bin. 'You and me, we need to get out there and make some friends. Everyone's getting into groups and there'll be no one left by lunchtime.'

Hilary nods. 'This feels like my first day of Year Seven.' She glances at me. 'I didn't like secondary school much.'

'Forget secondary school. This is a new start.'

She smiles. 'Yeah, you're right! But how do we do this? How do we make friends with complete strangers?'

'First we need to narrow down the field. Ever played Find A Friend?'

This is highly unlikely, as I've just invented it. In fact, I've never been much of a seeker-outer of friends, but right now it seems like a good idea, otherwise I might spend the next two years sitting in the corner of the common room with Hilary. She's clearly great, but too much one-on-one time gets a bit heavy for me.

Hilary looks excited. 'What do we do?'

'Look around the room and choose one person you could befriend. Obviously, you're going to have to use very shallow selection criteria.'

Hilary nods and her eyes skip from person to person. 'Well, there's one person I would *never* choose,' she says, pulling a face, then her eyes move on. 'OK. I've found my friend. Yes. Definitely.'

'Who is it?'

'That boy eating pasta salad.'

I follow her eyes and see a boy sitting by the pool table. He's got neat black hair and his knees are clamped together with a Tupperware box balanced on them.

'OK ... Why?'

'Because the salad looks home-made and I just saw him add salad dressing that he had brought *in a separate bottle.*' She's delighted by this detail.

'Salad-dressing boy it is. Out of curiosity, who was it that made you shiver with loathing?'

'That girl by the door.' Her eyes flick towards a girl who's laughing and holding a smoothie. 'Abbie Sweeney.'

'What's wrong with Abbie Sweeney?'

'She called me "smelly owl" for four years at St Cuthbert's. She dropped the "smelly" in Year Eleven, but, still, not very nice.'

I stare hard at Abbie Sweeney, committing her dip-dyed red hair, sprinkling of freckles and upturned nose to memory. Just let her try calling Hilary a smelly owl when I'm around … I'll call her a funky fox. No, that sounds too positive. Maybe a *fetid* fox …

'So what about you?' says Hilary, interrupting my dark thoughts. 'Who would you befriend?'

'Well, obviously not Abbie Sweeney.'

'Thanks!'

'Let's see …' My eyes sweep the room from left to right. 'Him.' I nod towards a boy who's sitting next to Hilary's salad-dressing boy.

'The redhead or the blond?'

'The dirty blond. I like his long fingers.'

'Long fingers must be your salad dressing.'

'I guess so,' I say, laughing. Then I stand up and brush the crumbs from my lap. 'Come on. We need to introduce ourselves to our new friends.'

'What?' Hilary's eyes go wide – in fact, if I'm totally honest, they look a little owlish. 'We're just going to go over there and … say hello?'

'That's it!'

I walk across the room, and, after a moment's hesitation, Hilary follows me.

'Hi!' I say, making the boys look up.

Hilary's boy holds a pasta spiral suspended in front of his mouth. He swallows and blinks.

'I'm Annie and this is Hilary, and out of everyone in the room we chose you to come and talk to!'

'An excellent choice,' says Long Fingers. Up close, I see that the rest of him is pretty appealing too – black specs, just the right amount of tight blue T-shirt and a big easy smile. 'I'm Jim, and this is Maliik – Mal for short.' Salad boy wiggles his pasta spiral. 'And that's Oliver.'

Oliver blurts out, 'I'm getting a drink,' and gets to his feet. 'Excuse me,' he says, as he edges past us.

'Sorry about Oli,' says Jim. 'We went to an all-boys' school and that's actually the longest conversation he's ever had with a woman.'

Woman, I think, enjoying how the word makes me feel.

'Not true,' Oliver calls over his shoulder. He's got one of those complexions that can go from milky white to red in a matter of seconds. Right now, it's on scarlet mode.

'Oh, yeah. He said "hello" to my mum once.'

Oliver walks off, shaking his head.

'I guess we might as well have Oliver's seat,' I say, and Hilary and I sit down.

34

Mal goes back to his salad and Jim starts chatting. Soon he's told us loads of stuff, like how they became friends because they were the only boys in their year who didn't like football and that Mal actually *does* like football, only he pretends not to so he can hang out with Oli and Jim.

'Oh, there's one thing you should know about Oli,' says Jim. 'He's got this obscene carrot addiction.'

Mal laughs into his salad.

'What about you, Jim?' I say. 'Anything that we should know about you?'

He sits back and smiles. 'Only that I have an obscene music collection – obscenely *good*, that is.' And then he's off on one, going on about house rhythms and funky basslines – or is it funky rhythms and house basslines?

Soon I'm wearing his Bang and Olufsen headphones and nodding away to … something. It's almost definitely techno.

I pass the headphones on to Hilary as Oliver reappears. He leans against the wall, opens his drink, then gets a carrot out of his bag. It's already peeled and wrapped in cling film.

When he sees us watching him, Oliver scowls. 'I'm not addicted,' he says. 'This is my first one today.'

Which makes us all burst out laughing. A girl sitting on a sofa next to us glances over, and, just like that, we've joined the Big Laughers.

SIX

I thought I might get stressed on my first day at college, and lost and definitely tired, but I didn't expect to enjoy myself so much. After five years of the same teachers, students and rules, I'm delighted by every new thing I encounter. The library lets you take out your own books in a machine! There's a shop in reception that sells tampons and pencil sharpeners! My sociology teacher tells us to call him Phil!

And so my first day passes in an exciting blur of new experiences and trying not to fall over.

My final lesson is psychology. After that, I get my wheelchair and head for the station. I bump into Hilary as I'm going down the hill – quite literally, as I creep up behind her and do it on purpose. We talk about our lessons and Hilary shares her pecan-pie-flavoured M&M's with me.

Just seven hours ago, I was coming up this hill on my own and now I'm sharing obscure sweets with an old friend from playgroup. This feels like the perfect end to the perfect day.

At the station, I meet up with Jackson. I don't get to hear about his day because the moment we get on the train, his phone rings and he starts talking to Amelia. I use this opportunity to carry on reading *Wuthering Heights*. The narrator, Lockwood, is having a bit of bad luck: he's been caught in a snowstorm, attacked by dogs and forced to stay the night in Heathcliff's house.

I'm totally hooked.

That is, until Jackson starts talking about salad in a loud voice.

'… *sky and hills mingled in one bitter whirl of wind and suffocating snow* …' I read.

'So this boy in my biology class bought a ham and salad baguette and all it had inside was a piece of ham and two bits of cucumber,' Jackson tells Amelia.

'… *it was so dark that I could not see the means of exit* …'

'I know! Salad has to be *at least* two things … lettuce, pepper, onion, tomato … No. Not coleslaw. That doesn't count …'

'… *two hairy monsters flew at my throat* …'

37

'I didn't know you like beetroot. I love beetroot! It tastes like metal, so when I eat it I pretend I'm eating *soft* metal.'

And that's when I give up reading and dedicate the rest of the journey to listening in on Jackson and Amelia's never-ending conversation. It's strangely soothing, especially when they try to say goodbye to each other.

'Bye ... OK ... Bye ... See you later ... No, you hang up ... OK ... Do it now ... You didn't hang up, did you?'

'Are you *sure* you said goodbye properly?' I ask when Jackson finally puts his phone away. 'Maybe you should ring her back and check.'

'Very funny,' he says. 'Just 'cause I'm not a lone wolf like you.'

I burst out laughing. 'A lone wolf? Where did that come from?'

He shrugs. 'Well, you've never been that into having friends, have you? I seem to remember you were the only person in our year group who turned up at the prom on their own.'

'Yeah, because I *chose* to! I could have sat in any number of pink limos if I'd wanted to. But I didn't. It's not my thing going round in a pack of girls.'

'You don't go round in a pack of anything.'

'That's right,' I say proudly, sitting back in my seat, 'but it doesn't mean I haven't got friends. I've got loads!

For example, Meg, Dara, Kiri, Elizabeth, Rose, Ed, Luke, *you* –'

'Name the last person you had over to your house.' He smiles like he's enjoying himself.

Honestly? It was probably Dara back in Year Ten, but I'm not telling Jackson that. 'We're sixteen, Jackson. We don't have people round to play any more. Anyway, why are you so worried about my friends all of a sudden?'

He shrugs. 'I'm not really. You were having a go at me about Amelia so I thought I'd return the favour.'

'Thank you very much,' I say, then I mime holding up a piece of paper and drawing a big cross on it.

'What are you doing?'

'Crossing you off my friend list,' I say.

Then Jackson tries to cross me off his friend list, only he uses a Sharpie and my arm. So I attempt to unfriend him on Facebook, but he fights me for my phone, I get the giggles and then an old man tells us off.

I spend the rest of the journey staring out of the window, because I know that if I even look at Jackson's silly face, I'll start laughing again.

And, of course, I think about what Jackson's just said.

He's probably right. I'm friendly with a lot of people, but there's no one I talk to every day or who I'd describe as a 'best friend'. I guess it's because at the start of secondary school I had a couple of operations and missed the moment when everyone got into groups. Also, I get tired in the evenings and at weekends, so sometimes it's easier not to make plans at all than to have to cancel them at the last minute and let people down.

But maybe it's time I made room in my life for a friend. Just a small one. With yellow glasses and round cheeks.

As we go down the station platform, I say to Jackson, 'I did make a new friend today, *actually*.'

'Oh, yeah,' he says, smiling. 'Congratulations. And what's this friend's name?'

'Hilary.'

'You so made that up,' Jackson says, shaking his head.

I give him a shove, and he gives me an even bigger shove back, but I'm in my wheelchair so I'm unshoveable.

The moment we get through the ticket barrier, I see Amelia standing outside W.H. Smith. She's all willowy, and her hair belongs on a shampoo ad, and she's jumping up and down with the excitement of being reunited with the one and only Jackson Carter.

'Say "hi" from me,' I say, then Jackson shoots off across the concourse, like a puppy that's been let off the lead. I watch as they throw their arms around each other.

No one's at the station to meet me, not even my mum – and for me that's the best feeling in the world.

SEVEN

I've nearly finished making dinner when Mum gets in. She drops her bag of marking on the floor then comes over and gives me a big hug. This is reckless as I'm draining spaghetti and I'm surrounded by steam and boiling water.

'My big *college* girl!' she says, squeezing me tight. She smells powerfully of school dinners and children. This is her Monday to Friday smell. Her weekend and holiday smell is Chanel N° 5.

'That's enough,' I say after I've endured a couple of seconds of hug. 'Please release me before this pasta goes mushy.'

Mum watches me with an eager look on her face as I stir the pesto into the pasta. 'So … How was your day, Annie? Did everything go well? What are your teachers like?'

I narrow my eyes. Mum's great. Really, I couldn't ask for a better one: she's funny, good at all the essential mum stuff (cakes, hot-water bottles, lifts) and she has an excellent haircut that makes her look like a feminine elf. But, like all mums, she can be a wee bit inquisitive.

'Have you washed your hands?' I say.

She looks at her hands. 'What's that got to do with anything?'

I put the bowls of pasta on the table. 'You've just spent the day wiping bottoms. You probably need to wash your hands with bleach.'

'I only wiped one bottom today,' she says, squirting soap on to her hands. 'Oh, and I cleaned up a bit of sick at milk time.'

'Revolting.'

Mum sits down and starts twirling spaghetti on to her fork. 'Now stop mucking around, Annie Demos, and tell me how your day went.'

'I didn't wipe anyone's bottom or clean up any sick, so, all in all, I'm guessing I had a pretty good day compared to yours.'

Mum shakes her head. 'No jokes. I want hard facts: who you met, details of *exactly* what you ate at lunch-time, the high points and low points of your day.'

I cover my pasta in Cheddar. 'I hung out with three boys: Jim, Oliver and Mal. Oliver likes eating carrots. I ate a rice salad at lunchtime and it was good. Actually, it was so good that it might have been the high point of the day.' Then, almost so I can see what it feels like, I add, 'And I met this girl, Hilary. I like her a lot. I think I might invite her round.'

Mum's eyes shoot up from her food. 'Great,' she says. 'Seriously, any time!' She'd love to quiz me about Hilary, but she knows me well enough to leave it at that.

We carry on eating as I describe my form group, then Mum asks, 'Any low points?' She says this casually, sprinkling more cheese on her pasta, but I know that she has been worrying about me all day.

'No low points,' I say, sidestepping the memory of Fab calling me an invalid. 'I didn't fall over, I received a totally predictable amount of stares and I got the train fine. I feel crazy tired now, but I don't care because I loved my lessons. In psychology we learnt about the strangest experiment involving a monkey and a fake mum-monkey made of wire.'

Mum looks at me as she sucks in a long bit of spaghetti, and then I notice she's blinking at the same time.

'Mum … Are you *crying*? All I did was go to college. That's not worthy of tears!'

43

The last bit of spaghetti whips into her mouth and she shakes her head. 'I'm not crying. My contact lenses are wandering about – I'm trying to get them back in position.'

'Oh ... well, good.'

She jabs her fork at me. 'You'll have to do more than get a train and eat a rice salad to make me cry, young lady.'

'Win a medal at the Paralympics?'

'No ... It would need to be something that made me feel *really* proud.'

'Win *The Great British Bake Off?*' This is Mum's favourite programme in the world and watching it is a sacred experience for her. She even has this little ritual where she gets in her pyjamas, makes a cup of tea, then opens a packet of cheese and onion crisps. I'm not allowed to speak to her until the credits are rolling and I definitely don't get any of the crisps.

'That would do it,' she says, smiling at the thought. 'Paul Hollywood squeezing your buns ...'

I shake my head. 'You just went too far.'

'Sorry,' she says with a grin. She doesn't look sorry at all.

EIGHT

After dinner, I disappear up to my bedroom.

I'm exhausted, but the moment I shut my bedroom door, say 'hi' to my rats and turn on my music, a feeling of lightness sweeps through me.

My room might be a mess of make-up and trainers, and contain a ridiculously large rats' cage, but it's my sanctuary. I'm not just tired because my muscles ache; I'm tired because all day I've been putting on a stellar performance of Being Annie. Laughing, radiating self-confidence, meeting every stare with a smile. Everyone makes an effort when they meet people for the first time, but being disabled means I've got to work that little bit harder. It takes a serious amount of pink lipstick, bravado and bling to remind people that the way I walk is only part of who I am.

But here in my room, I can let all that go.

I shut the curtains, take off my make-up and pull on my softest tracksuit bottoms and a pair of fluffy socks. Luckily, Mum understands that I need a lot of downtime, and she never tries to guilt-trip me into hanging out with her. Except on Eurovision night – that's the one evening when downtime is banned.

The whole time I'm moving round my room, my rats, Mabel and Alice, are peering over the edge of their hammock, watching me with their beady black eyes.

'Freedom!' I say, as I open their cage door.

Straight away, Mabel shoots out of the cage and scampers under my bed, but Alice is more sociable and runs on to my shoulder and sniffs my face. Alice smells like honey on toast … with a hint of rat.

'Hello, beautiful,' I say.

I pick her off my shoulder, lay her on her back and tickle her soft, white tummy. She grabs hold of my thumb in her tiny hands and we share a moment of intensely rewarding eye contact. I really do love my girls.

After I've cleaned their cage and put them away, I curl up on my bed and open *Wuthering Heights*. I ache from my shoulders right down to the backs of my legs, but as I read my whole body kind of melts. This is another reason I love reading. Compared to participating in real life, the experience of opening a book and stepping into someone else's life requires no effort at all.

And right now, Lockwood's life is mucked up.

He's staying the night at Wuthering Heights, and as he reaches out of a window a tiny icy hand grabs him and won't let go. It's seriously scary. The hand belongs to a ghost … or maybe it doesn't. Maybe Lockwood's dreaming. He can't tell because he's in that weird halfway place between being asleep and awake.

Just like me …

Even though it's just gone ten, I turn out my light and pull my duvet over me. Then I lie in the dark, Alice and Mabel snuffling around their cage, my mind bouncing between *Wuthering Heights* and my day at Cliffe College: I see my friends, Hilary the owl, and Jim with his huge headphones and Oliver with his beautiful red hair; then Heathcliff storms in, with his dark glower, only to be replaced by Fabian Kaczka with his fringed scarf and Bombay Sapphire stare.

NINE

When I get to college the next day, fully recharged and ready to go, Fab's stare is the first thing I see.

He's standing by the main gates, legs astride, arms folded, looking like a bouncer. He's still wearing his black trainers, but today he's paired them with running shorts and a striped shirt that's loosely buttoned and showing a lot of chest. It's really hard to tell if he's rocking an incredible mismatched look or simply got dressed in the dark.

'Annie!' he shouts, beckoning me over. 'Come here.' The way he's positioned himself right by the gates makes me wonder if he's been lying in wait for me.

My first instinct is to ignore him. I'm not sure I want to start the day with an awkward conversation, and I'm in my wheelchair. If he thought I was an 'invalid' when I was walking, what will he think now? Maybe he'll crouch down like he's talking to a child – or, worse, try and push me.

'Annie!' he bellows. '*Annie!*'

With a sigh, I turn in his direction. Sometimes it's best to meet life's challenges head-on.

'ANNIE!'

Plus, he's obviously not giving up.

The moment I reach Fab, he dumps a large box on my lap. 'I would be grateful if you could help me, please. Just find the correct baguette and pass them to my customers.'

Confused, I peer into the box and see that it's stuffed full of cellophane-wrapped baguettes. 'Fab, what are you on about?'

'The baguette I had in the canteen yesterday was small and it was dry so I have made better ones.'

The baguettes all have stickers labelled with Fab's loopy handwriting: *sausage*, *cheese and tom*, *zapiekanka*. I notice the *zapiekanka* ones are still hot and oozing cheese.

'You do know that the college won't like you selling baguettes?' I say. 'You're nicking their business.'

'Then they should make better baguettes,' he says with a shrug. 'Anyway, it is just for today. I had to get up very early to make them. Too early.' Then, before I can mention trading licenses or hygiene laws, or point out that I don't actually want to help him, he starts shouting at the top of his voice: 'Fresh *baguettes*! Half the price of the canteen, double the taste. *Zapiekanka*: one hundred per cent vegetarian!'

People stare at him, alarmed, but this doesn't put him off. 'Hey, my friend,' he says, stepping in front of a boy who's simply trying to walk into college. 'Got any lunch? Get a baguette right here!' Then I notice that people are staring at me too, assuming that I'm part of Fab's baguette business.

'Er, Fab,' I say, 'I think I might –'

'BAGUETTES!' he bellows. 'BAGUETTES! When they are gone, they are gone!'

Now, this is a new experience for me. Usually, in any given group of teenagers, I'm the loud, confident one, but Fab's market-trader act is making me feel a little, well, *embarrassed*. With alarm, I wonder if this is what it's like hanging out with me. No, I decide – my loud moments are well judged and funny. Whereas Fab's are just, well, *loud*.

'How much are they?' Finally, Fab has succeeded at drawing in one of the jocks from my form group.

'To you, one pound fifty,' Fab says, then he runs through the fillings.

The boy buys two sausage baguettes and that's all it takes to make a group of girls stop to see what's going on. This small crowd attracts others and soon I'm surrounded on all sides, with hands reaching into the box for baguettes, and people shouting 'sausage' and 'cheese' in my face.

And that's when I decide I've had enough of being Fab's table.

'Hold this,' I say to a girl, passing her the box, then I push my way out of the crowd. I pop out on the other side and almost run into Jim.

'Hello,' he says, pulling off his headphones. If he's surprised to see me in a wheelchair, he hides it well. 'What's going on?'

'Baguettes is what's going on. A boy from my English class is selling them.'

'How curious,' he says, then he nods towards the main entrance. 'You coming in?'

Before I have a chance to reply, Fab's hand lands on my shoulder. 'Annie, where are you going?'

'Into college.'

'But I haven't given you my present. That's why I called you over.' He pulls a bunch of battered flowers out from behind his back. 'For you,' he says formally, and again I get one of his bows.

I stare at the big bloomy flowers and feel a blush creep over my face. The flowers are huge and red and pink, and seem – to my untrained eye – ridiculously *romantic*. Why on earth is he giving them to me?

51

Fab mistakes my focused stare for one of botanical curiosity. 'They're dahlias,' he says. 'My mum grows them on her allotment. She brought the seeds all the way from Poland, which is why they are extremely beautiful.'

He bends over me to tweak at the flowers, pulling out one that's half snapped. I see an amused smile spread across Jim's face.

Fab clears his throat. 'Annie, these flowers are to say "sorry" for my rudeness yesterday. I have been on the internet and I have discovered a lot about language and disability. My mum always says words should be weighed and not counted, and I will be remembering that in the future.'

'Right ...'

'Please have them,' says Fab, pushing the flowers towards me.

Other students are staring at us now and some are smiling like they're witnessing a magical romantic moment.

Quickly, I take the dahlias and drop them on my lap. 'Look, Fab, thanks and everything, but don't beat yourself up about what you said. I'd rather you just talked to me normally than worried about saying the wrong thing.'

A smile spreads across his face. 'I would *love* to talk to you! When?'

OK. That wasn't what I meant. 'Later,' I say.

'What's your number?' he asks, whipping out his phone. 'We can arrange it.'

He stands there, looking at me expectantly. This boy does not give up.

'Give me your number,' I say. 'I can never remember mine.' This is an obvious lie, but Fab doesn't seem to mind. This way I get to decide if I contact him or not.

As Fab reels off his number, a girl wanders over with a baguette. 'Who do I pay for this?'

'I must go,' Fab says, then he grabs my hand, squeezes it and goes back to his customers.

I stare at my hand and laugh.

'He is one weird dude,' says Jim, shaking his head.

We walk towards college and, for a moment, I think about letting Jim's 'weird' comment go. I mean, didn't I just say people shouldn't worry too much about saying the wrong thing?

But I've never been much good at letting things go.

'You think he's *weird*, Jim? Do you prefer people to be normal?'

He laughs. 'Not really. Look who I hang out with ... And I do believe that weird is the new normal.'

'You so got that off a T-shirt. I hope you don't own it.'

'Actually, I got it off a mug. My sister owns it, which is odd because she's the most normal person I know.'

'My mum once got me a mug that says, "World's Greatest Disabled Person".'

'Seriously?'

I look up at him as I push through the double doors. 'She's got a good sense of humour.'

We join the crush of students. 'I wonder if I could get one that says, "World's Greatest Abled Person"?' he muses.

'Jim, you can get *anything* on a mug.'

We spend the next few minutes thinking up bad mug slogans. My favourites are: 'Am I a mug?', 'Keep calm and carry on mugging' and 'Mmm, this tea's lovely … Feeling s*mug*'.

Although Jim says that won't fit on a mug.

So s*mug*.

We part at the lift. 'See you at break?' I say. Jim's so laidback, I feel I can say this without sounding like a stalker, or, worse, as if I can't handle being on my own.

'Maybe,' he says, raising one eyebrow, 'unless you've arranged to meet up for a chat and a sausage baguette with Fab.'

I open my mouth to have the last word, but just then the lift doors slide shut.

Man, he timed that well.

TEN

At break, I notice that already different groups of students are claiming corners and sofas in the common room. In a way, this is like school, only the groups here seem more fuzzy round the edges. For example, the alpha group at school was made up solely of beautiful sporty types, but the group who have taken the blue sofa by the iPod dock – definitely the best place in the room – seems more inclusive. They're all still confident and, on the whole, beautiful, but I'm seeing vintage clothing, hats, at least one beard *and* a girl crocheting.

This is an interesting development …

I look around for Hilary and almost bump into Georgina Carr, looking lost.

Her eyes light up when she sees me. 'Annie! How are you doing?'

'Yeah, good,' I say cautiously, because being treated like a human being by Georgina is a bit odd. Over by the pool table, I spot Hilary, Mal and Oliver.

'*Annie!*' calls Hilary, waving madly.

I look back at Georgina and she looks so lonely I have to say, 'Coming to sit down?'

Maybe it's Hilary's charity shop specs, or possibly it's Mal's school shoes that he's wearing with ironed jeans, but something about my new friends puts Georgina off. 'No, you're all right,' she says, wrinkling her nose. 'I'm just going … this way.' And she wanders off in search of someone 'better'.

I wonder if I should tell her that the sporty types have taken over the picnic tables outside, but they're not *beautiful* sporty types – they're just people studying sports science – and I don't think this would be acceptable to Georgina either. I watch her walk away, her eyes flicking anxiously from side to side.

For five years, I've wanted to see Georgina knocked off her pedestal and forced to experience what life is like for people born without flawless skin and the ability to run fast and bounce a ball at the same time. I watch as she takes out her phone and stares at the screen, nibbling her lip. I just didn't realise that when it happened I'd feel so sorry for her.

I weave through people, dodging pool cues and rucksacks, and sit next to Hilary.

'So, guess what?' she says.

'What?'

'Oliver is a part-time pest controller!'

'I really don't think I would have guessed that,' I say, laughing.

Oliver shrugs off this revelation and starts to discuss his poisons, vermin and 'clients'.

'He's got business cards and everything,' says Hilary.

'Hang on,' I say. 'You actually *own* a business?'

He ducks his head modestly. 'Just a small one.'

Yesterday I was laughing at Oliver for having a carrot addiction and now I'm being told he's an entrepreneur. Maybe I should start eating raw carrots …

As Oliver describes clients who've encountered rats in their toilets (while they've been *in the act*), all of his awkwardness from yesterday slips away and even his blush dies down. I suppose, as a vegetarian rat lover, I should find his job disturbing, but he talks with such animation it's hard not to get swept along in his enthusiasm for getting rid of living creatures.

'Last night, I was working in an attic when I found a nest of baby rats in a suitcase,' he says.

'I've got two pet rats,' I say. 'Alice and Mabel.'

Oliver looks up at me and with complete seriousness says, 'Mr Rat is an exceptionally intelligent and resourceful creature.'

This is all the encouragement I need to get out my phone and show him far too many pictures of Alice and Mabel being both intelligent and resourceful.

'Look,' I say. 'In this one Alice is opening a drawer and, because she's lazy, Mabel is waiting for her to do it and then she's going to steal the bit of cheese!'

That's when Jim appears and pulls up a chair. 'I am the bearer of good news,' he says, getting some cards out of his bag. 'In three weeks this girl in my maths group, Sophie, is having an eighteenth birthday party and you're all invited.'

'It's at the East Bay Hotel,' I say, taking an invitation. 'That's near where I live.'

'How come we're invited?' asks Hilary.

'Her mum's the manager at the hotel so she's got this massive function room for free. Only problem is, now she needs to fill it so she's handing out invitations to everyone.'

On the front of the invitation is a photo of a girl pouting, with *Sophie is 18 and MAD FOR IT!!* printed below her face.

'But we don't know Mad For It Sophie,' I say.

Jim shrugs. 'Doesn't matter. Everyone's going.'

'I think we should go,' Hilary says, nudging me.

'Maybe, but I might be too tired,' I say, trying to predict how I'll feel in three weeks' time. Plus I can't quite remember what access is like at the East Bay Hotel. Most people my age do things like getting the train, walking round college every day and going to parties without thinking, but for me it's hard work and involves a lot of planning.

'Right,' says Hilary. 'See how you feel.'

Suddenly, I realise I've been here before, at that point when I firmly but kindly keep someone at a distance. If I don't commit to this party, Hilary will find someone else to go with. We'll still be friends, but the ties between us will be slightly loosened. Almost with surprise, I realise I don't want this to happen.

'I'm sure it will be fine,' I say, and her eyes light up. Then, before I can change my mind, I add, 'And if you want, you can come round to my place to get ready … And stay the night.'

Hilary's eyes double in size and she actually hugs me. I feel a bit giddy. *Take that, Jackson Carter!* Not only have I invited someone over to my house, but now we're sealing the deal with a hug. Which is *exactly* the kind of thing friends do!

Hilary lets me go and says, 'It will be like at playgroup: you and me, causing mayhem together.'

'Painting stuff with Tippex,' I say, 'naked bouncing.'

Oliver's face quickly goes a deep shade of red and we all watch, fascinated, as the blush spreads out down his neck and across his ears.

'Are you blushing because Annie said "naked bouncing"?' asks Jim.

Oliver shakes his head. 'No.'

'Naked bouncing,' Jim says. 'Naked bouncing … naked bouncing … naked bouncing.'

But Oliver has regained his composure and is staring at Jim stony-faced.

'Hello,' says Jim, looking across the room. 'It's your friend, Annie.'

Fab has walked into the common room and is standing in the doorway. He surveys the room, taking his time, sipping the drink he's holding. For a moment, I'm sure he's looking for me so we can have our chat, but then he clocks the iPod-dock hoggers in the corner and walks towards them. I have this sudden lurch in my stomach, like when you want to stop a child falling over, because even though Fab is so tall and confident, I just don't know what the Hoggers will make of him.

I can't hear what he's saying, so I just have to watch as

he attempts a bit of matey handshaking and as eyebrows are raised and smiles are exchanged behind his back.

'You know him?' whispers Hilary.

'He's in my English class,' I say. 'He's friendly … Maybe too friendly?'

'I think he's a BFG,' says Hilary.

A Big Friendly Giant. I guess that does sort of sum him up.

'Well, the BFG gave Annie flowers,' says Jim. 'He's her *boyfriend*.'

He drawls this last word, and I feel a rush of irritation that he's making something out of nothing. I feel something else too – the kind of panic you get when you're eleven and someone says, 'My mate fancies you,' and you realise you're in a situation you never asked to be in.

Hilary only makes things worse by going, 'Ahhh!'

I need to put a stop to this right away. Having a boyfriend is so far off what I want right now it's not even funny. I mean, I just had problems committing to a sleepover!

'Sorry to disappoint you both,' I say, 'but I'm not interested in going out with Fab.'

Over by the blue sofa, Fab fiddles with the precious iPod.

'Why not?' asks Hilary. 'He's nice.'

'I'm sure he is, but I like my freedom far too much to become someone's girlfriend.' I guess I say this a bit too passionately because Jim's eyes widen with amusement. To change the subject, I say, 'OK. Guess what song he's putting on.'

'Rap,' says Mal, 'or hip-hop.'

'No way,' says Jim. 'Heavy metal. Bad, Polish heavy metal.'

'Or Adele, "Rolling in the Deep"?' suggests Hilary.

And at that moment, Adele singing 'Rolling in the Deep' sweeps through the common room.

We look at Hilary.

'Are you a witch?' I say. 'How did you know that?'

She grins. 'I sat next to him in French this morning. We had to interview each other and he said it's his favourite song.'

Now Fab's sitting next to a girl with white-blonde hair and pale pink lips. Together they're belting out 'Rolling in the Deep' and the eye-rolling from the rest of the group seems to have halted. Has Fab entered the lion's den and survived?

The song ends, and as Mal starts telling us about his guitar teacher (apparently he eats kebabs during the lessons, but he's cheap), I watch Fab get up, study the posters on a noticeboard, find some that have fallen on the floor and then pin them back in place. A minute later, he's leaning over the hatch into the coffee shop and chatting to the woman who works there. He makes a sweeping hand gesture which knocks over a pile of shortbread, and when he attempts to help tidy up, he's ushered away.

He takes one last look round the room, then strolls towards the exit. Suddenly, he rushes forward to hold the door open for Miss Caudle. As she walks past, cookie balanced on her mug of coffee, Fab does one of his little bows. Miss Caudle beams up at him and I'm almost certain she *bats her lashes*.

Miss Caudle wears an *Ask me about my feminist agenda* badge. Next time I see her, I'm going to take her up on that.

ELEVEN

When I walk into English on Wednesday, Fab's already sitting at our desk waiting for me.

'Annie,' he says, beckoning me over. 'I need to talk to you.'

'Sounds urgent,' I say.

Once again, when I sit down, I'm forced up against the window by Fab's rather relaxed way of sitting. Today he's wearing a disappointingly conventional blue T-shirt, but who knows what he's got on his bottom half.

I'm half expecting him to ask me why I haven't messaged him, but instead he says, 'I want to talk to you about *Wuthering Heights*.'

I pull my copy out of my bag. 'What about it? Everyone is so messed up and controlling. Especially Heathcliff.'

'Ah!' he says, holding up a finger. 'That is *exactly* what I want to talk about: *Heathcliff*.'

I get out my laptop. 'Well, he's not a nice person, but I still find myself rooting for him, you know?'

'Yes,' says Fab. 'He is both good and bad, but do you think he is sexy?'

I burst out laughing. '*Sexy?*'

He pulls out his phone and taps on the screen. 'Look, I found his name in a list of the Hottest Male Book Characters. Heathcliff comes second after Mr Darcy in *Pride and Prejudice* and before Count Vronsky in *Anna Karenina*.'

'Well, I suppose he is a bit sexy, what with all his brooding and scowling.' I shrug. 'Everyone loves a bad boy.'

Fab continues looking at me. 'I know,' he says, drumming his fingers on the desk, 'and this is wrong. Everyone should love a *kind*, respectful boy who treats girls well and … cares for them and –'

'Opens doors?' I suggest, smiling.

'*Exactly!* A bad boy like Heathcliff does not deserve to be on the Hottest Characters list.'

'Well, I suppose bad boys keep life interesting. I'm not sure we'd be reading *Wuthering Heights* if Heathcliff just went around opening doors for people and being kind.'

His fingers stop moving and he fixes me with his intense stare. 'But is that what *you* believe, Annie? That kind is less important than interesting?'

'*Me?*' This conversation is getting stranger and stranger. 'I guess so. I love all the scenes that Heathcliff is in. That's when all the exciting stuff happens.'

For some reason my words make Fab sigh and shake his head, but I'm saved from any more Heathcliff analysis by Miss Caudle starting the lesson. She asks us how much of the book we've managed to read and, as Fab and I are the furthest ahead, she tells us to sum up the plot for the rest of the class.

'Come, Annie,' says Fab, jumping to his feet and striding to the front of the room.

I'm fairly certain Miss Caudle just wanted us to do this briefly, from our seats, but I still get up and follow him.

'OK,' says Fab, addressing the class, 'here is what happens. A rich man brings home an orphan, Heathcliff, and the rich man's daughter, Catherine, loves Heathcliff from the moment she sets eyes on him –'

'Er, no, she doesn't,' I interrupt. 'She spits on him.'

Fab shakes his head. 'Yes, but a few days later, they are devoted to each other and are so in love that nothing can keep them apart!' Fab says these last words with such theatrical relish that the class starts to laugh.

'Right, they're so *in love*,' I say, 'that Catherine marries a richer man and then Heathcliff marries her sister-in-law as some sort of sick punishment.' I've been doing a bit of

66

research online. 'Oh, and then he makes Catherine's daughter marry his son. Nothing says *love* quite like forcing your dead ex-girlfriend's daughter to marry your son.'

Fab turns to face me and raises a finger. 'Annie, you are looking at this in the wrong way.'

'Oh, am I?'

The students' eyes flick between us as we talk, like people watching a ball at a tennis match.

He nods and the finger wags. 'Yes. You see, Catherine and Heathcliff's love for each other is so powerful it goes beyond what other people understand. It is almost super-natural.' He rushes to find a page he's dog-eared in his book. 'Catherine says, "I *am* Heathcliff". They aren't two people – they are one person joined by love.' He snaps the book shut. 'It is a deeply romantic idea.'

I laugh. 'Er … No, it's not! Losing your identity in a relationship is a deeply creepy and controlling idea. All through *Wuthering Heights* Catherine tries to escape and be free, but she can only attempt that through marriage, so she can never truly escape.' I glance at Miss Caudle's feminist badge. 'And nothing's really changed. Women still see the label "girlfriend" as a sign of success and the one route to happiness – they're just as trapped as Catherine.'

In the front row of desks, I see a girl busy texting and a boy struggling not to yawn.

'This book is about the power of love,' says Fab. 'From the moment Heathcliff and Catherine meet, they are *bratnimi duszami*, soulmates, and their love is a source of happiness in their lives.'

'No, it isn't,' I say. 'It makes them *miserable*.'

Fab sighs deeply, like I'm missing the point, and I roll my eyes to make it clear that it's definitely *him* who's missing the point.

'Could you both be right?' suggests Miss Caudle.

Well, probably, but I don't feel like agreeing with Fab.

'Nope,' I say. 'I don't see *love* in this book. I see women struggling to be free of the constraints society puts on them.'

'Heathcliff is "owned" by Cathy too,' says Fab. He's stopped looking at the rest of the class and is just looking at me. 'And society stops him from doing what he wants.'

'Ah, so I'm right: "love" traps the characters.'

Fab shakes his head. 'Love *frees* the characters.'

Miss Caudle is so delighted with our argument that she gives us a round of applause. 'It's wonderful to see you reacting with such passion to the book,' she says.

I wouldn't say the rest of the class are sharing our 'passion'. They're looking at us with a mixture of boredom and confusion. I guess our plot summary wasn't very

68

helpful because Miss Caudle puts an account of the first three chapters on the board and tells us to make notes.

Fab and I sit down.

'Love,' whispers Fab, 'is an adventure!'

I snort, and Miss Caudle shoots me a look.

'A trip on the *Titanic* was supposed to be an adventure,' I whisper back. 'Look how that ended up.'

A few minutes later, while Miss Caudle is still talking to the class, Fab slides his notebook across to me, the one where he records English words and phrases. He's written: *At least the passengers had four good days.*

I laugh and shake my head, and I wonder where this boy, who says things like this, but who also believes in love and kindness and goes round handing out flowers, has come from. I don't think it's anything to do with him being Polish. Lius and Dan at my old school were Polish, and I never saw them doing anything romantic ... Although once Dan did nick an Appletiser from the canteen for his girlfriend.

Twenty seconds later, Fab gets a text. I watch him pull out his phone, read the message, smile, then slip his phone back in his pocket.

I know exactly what the message says because I just sent it: **Now that was a naughty thing to say. Congratulations ... you just joined the bad boys!**

TWELVE

The next couple of weeks at college fly by. This is partly because I'm having so much fun with Hilary and the boys, but it's also because I'm loving my English lessons so much – or, to be precise, I'm loving arguing with Fab so much.

A curious consequence of being disabled is that people often agree with me, even if they don't actually agree with me at all. They assume my life is hard and they don't want to knock me down any further by telling me I'm wrong about something.

Fab doesn't buy into this idea. In fact, he never gives me an inch and he challenges everything I say. This literary bickering even continues out of lessons via texts.

Me: OMG. Heathcliff's just dug up Cathy's body. Sick!

Fab: Surely romantic?

Me: Errr ...

Fab: Joke.

Today, when Miss Caudle tells us our homework is to work in pairs making collages that explore themes, Fab and I start arguing straight away. We're happy working together – it's the theme we can't agree on.

'It has to be "Foreignness or the Other",' says Fab, pointing at the whiteboard. 'We have a lot of expertise in that area.'

'Speak for yourself,' I say. 'I want to do the supernatural. I was a Goth between the ages of thirteen and fourteen, and I have a lot of gloomy craft supplies that need using up.'

'Like what?'

'Ghost stamps, black puffy paint ...'

'I think you are not taking this homework seriously enough.'

I laugh. 'Well, I think you're taking it too seriously!'

'Fab 'n' Annie!' Miss Caudle calls from the front of the class.

I really wish she wouldn't call us this. It began as a joke because she had to ask us to be quiet so often, then the rest of the class shortened it to 'Fannie'. Not only have I unwittingly become part of a supercouple, but our/my nickname is Fannie. Marvellous.

'Yes, Miss *Cuddle*?' I say pointedly.

'You two are doing love.'

'*What*? But that was my last choice, miss!'

'Sorry, but it's the only theme left. While you two were arguing about it, the others got taken.'

'That is perfect, Miss Cuddle,' says Fab, stretching back in his seat and putting his hands behind his head. 'It was my second choice. We will make an excellent love collage together.'

'Fannie are so adorable!' cries out Romilly, and I'm forced to throw my Tic Tac box at her.

'So, Annie,' says Fab, 'when shall we make our love collage?'

I shrug. 'After school some time?'

'Yes,' he says, 'at my house. It is just a few minutes away on the bus, and my mother works at Staples and recently brought home a very large piece of card.'

That wasn't what I meant. 'Couldn't you just bring it into college?'

He frowns and shakes his head. 'No. It is *very* large. How about after school tomorrow?'

I consider his suggestion for a moment. Obviously, Fannie meeting up at Fab's house might encourage some silly comments from the class, but it will probably be the easiest way to do the homework, and I've always enjoyed having a snoop round other people's homes.

'OK,' I say. 'I'll see if my mum can pick me up from your place.'

'And I will get my mother to buy some glue and big pens.'

'Cutest. Thing. Ever.' We look up to see Romilly grinning over at us.

She's already got my Tic Tacs – and appears to be eating them – so this time I'm forced to chuck my fluffy pencil case at her.

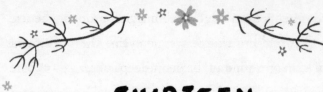

THIRTEEN

When Fab meets me outside college the next day, he tells me that he's going to pay for my bus ticket.

'You really don't need to do that,' I say.

'I don't want this to be any trouble for you. It is kind of you to come all the way to my house.'

'I'm not sure about *kind*. I live twenty miles away from college. You live two miles away. It's just the logical thing to do.'

He smiles. 'In that case, thank you, Annie, for being so logical.'

Suddenly, Fab leaps into the road and waves his arms around to flag down the bus. I'm fairly certain a raised finger would have done the trick, but Fab likes big gestures.

The bus is packed full of schoolchildren and shoppers – every seat is taken, and the wheelchair space is filled with two buggies. Sitting behind the buggies are two women; when the younger one notices me eyeing the pushchairs, she says, 'Sorry, there's babies asleep in there,' before turning back to talk to her friend.

Round here, wheelchairs have priority over push-chairs. In theory. I suppose I'm a bit of a grey area because I'm not confined to my wheelchair, although, after a day spent walking round college, I don't think I can stand.

'You're blocking the exit,' the bus driver tells me helpfully.

I look up, and the whole bus looks down, trying to keep themselves out of this awkward situation I'm causing. Although I'm not causing it. There is a space on this bus for me, but two babies are already in it.

Annoyance that I've been put in this situation flares up inside me. Fab steps forward to speak, but I put my hand on his arm.

'I can sort this out,' I say. I turn to the bus driver. 'You're not going to ask them to fold their buggies, are you? You're expecting me to do it.'

He keeps his hands on the steering wheel and his eyes fixed on the road ahead of him. 'Sorry, love. I just need to get this bus moving. Another one will be along in a few minutes.'

I shake my head. 'I'm not getting off this bus,' I say,

then, feeling the impatient, curious eyes of all the passengers on me, I get to my feet and fold up my chair. I hand it to Fab, who pushes it behind the buggies.

'Careful!' snaps the older mum.

Before I've even had a chance to ask someone to move, the bus roars into life. I grab the pole to stop myself from falling and that's when I notice where the priority seating is.

I might not to want to disturb the babies in front of a bus full of people, but I've got no problem disturbing their mums.

'Please can I have one of your seats?' I ask.

The younger mum blinks at me and stares. 'What?'

My heart speeds up and I hold on tight to the pole. 'You're sitting in a priority seat that's reserved for people who are elderly, disabled or pregnant, and I'm disabled.'

The two women study me suspiciously, looking me up and down, then the younger one sighs and says, 'Fine.' Then, oh so slowly, she gets to her feet.

I squeeze in next to her friend, and for the next few minutes the women are glued to their phones, sharing secret smiles and glances.

I'm fairly certain they're texting about me, so I keep my eyes on the window and try to project the strongest couldn't-care-less vibes possible, putting my shoulders back, yawning, smiling to myself. But it's hard, because of course I do care about having to fight for the right to get on a bus just like everyone else.

Suddenly my phone buzzes with a message from Fab.

What a couple of dupki.

I don't know what *dupki* means, but I'm guessing it's not nice.

Massive dupki, I text back.

I watch as he reads my message, then his eyes meet mine, and he gives me the briefest of smiles. He's too polite to make the women feel uncomfortable.

I settle back in my seat and take a sip of water, not faking being relaxed now. The women are still frantically tapping away on their phones, but I just let them, and what they're doing, wash over me because they're really not worth worrying about. Plus their babies have just woken up and are screaming their heads off.

Ha, ha, ha!

FOURTEEN

F ab lives in a small, square terraced house, with a small, square front garden stuffed full of the same flowers he gave me.

'My mother is at work,' he says, letting me in and ushering me into the kitchen.

It's as immaculate as the front garden, and arranged on the table is the much-discussed piece of Large Card and various craft items: glue, scissors, pens. Sweet. He must have got it all ready before he came into college this morning.

Fab pours us each a glass of squash, then we sit at the table, sipping our drinks. An awkward silence falls over us.

'I'm sorry about what happened on the bus,' Fab says, looking at me.

'It wasn't your fault.'

'No, but it was me who made you get the bus.'

'Yeah, but you didn't put the *dupki* on the bus. Forget about it.' I say this firmly, because I can sense Fab's teetering on the edge of trying to talk to me about my cerebral palsy, and I'm really not in the mood for that right now. What I'm in the mood for is some serious crafting. To make this clear to Fab, I pull a Tesco bag out of my rucksack.

'I've got all my love stuff in here,' I say, shaking out the bag.

Pieces of paper, scraps of fabric, and bits and bobs spill over the table. I show him the pictures of erupting volcanoes and storms that I tore out of Mum's *National Geographic* magazines.

'I've also cut out anything that symbolises being trapped: walls, chains, bars. Oh, look: I got a picture of a tower with no doors, on a cliff, surrounded by the sea! And I cut out these words from a newspaper.' I spread them out in front of me, making a sort of grim poem. '*Lost, hate, torn, assault, missing, scared, beat, agony,*' I read. 'Those last two came from an advert that said, "*New Way to Beat Agony of Piles*".'

'Ah,' he says, eyeing my heap of misery. 'I think maybe we have different views of love.'

Then he tips out the shoebox he's set on the table and it's like Clintons Cards on Valentine's Day: there are hearts (*lots* of hearts), flowers, rainbows, pouting lips, birds, bees and entwined couples. He's even got hold of some heart-shaped sequins. Like me, he's cut out words, but his are: *love, kiss, passion, strength, hope* and *touch*.

'Just a bit,' I say, sifting through them. I hold one up. '*Tender?* Fab, who's tender in *Wuthering Heights?*'

'Heathcliff is tender when he gives Catherine a lock of his hair twisted with her own.'

'But she's dead. He puts it on her corpse.'

Fab does one of his expansive shrugs, declaring, 'It is still tender. A little creepy, but tender.'

After two hours, and lots of cutting and sticking, we've produced a rather fine collage. We basically do half each and have fun arguing about which side the quotes should go on. In the end, we have to compromise with: '*Whatever our souls are made of, his and mine are the same*' and put it slap bang in the middle. I stick a pair of handcuffs on my side, and Fab retaliates by sticking an entwined lock of hair on his side. I don't even ask him where he got the hair from.

After we've tidied up, we've still got ten minutes until Mum's supposed to arrive, so I ask to see Fab's bedroom.

'My mother wouldn't like it,' he says, hesitating at the foot of the stairs.

'Well, I won't tell her if you don't,' I say. Then I add, 'They say eyes are supposed to be the windows to the soul, but I think bedrooms are far more revealing.'

He considers this for a moment then says, 'OK,' and leads the way upstairs. 'But if my mother comes back you must pretend you are using the toilet.'

After a painful walk up the stairs – the price I must pay for my curiosity – Fab pushes open his bedroom door, and I step into a neat and organised room.

One wall is taken up entirely with books, which are arranged alphabetically, and the Polish flag is pinned above a carefully made bed. On the window sill are the various caps and hats Fab wears into college and a pile of folded scarves. Everything is ordered and tidy: from the shoes lined up beneath the radiator, to a collection of photos stuck to the side of the wardrobe.

'My Polish friends and family,' Fab says, nodding at the photos.

Then I see another photo. It's the only one on a chest of drawers and it's also the only one in a frame. It's a wedding photo. The bride is wearing a billowing veil and gazing up at the groom.

'Are they your mum and dad?' I ask, and Fab nods.

Some bits and pieces are displayed around the photo: a Swiss army knife, a little metal box, a white egg covered in blue circles. Something about how precisely they've been placed next to the photo tells me these are special things.

'My father lives in Poland,' says Fab.

That's all. He doesn't tell me if his mum and dad are divorced, or why he's living with his mum and not his dad.

Fab asks me direct questions all the time, but even though I'd like to know more about his family, I don't say anything.

Instead, I say, 'You have your dad's eyes.'

'And his height.'

'Yep. You definitely don't get that from your mum.'

Fab's still hovering in the doorway, watching me. 'So,' he says, 'what has my room revealed about my soul?'

'That it craves order, which is not what I was expecting at all. At college you seem very ... spontaneous.'

He spreads his hands wide and smiles. 'I am a man of mystery! What is your bedroom like?'

'Messy, full of rats and chaotic,' I say, 'and yet I'm a bit of a control freak.' I take one last look around me and I see that the blanket at the end of his bed is folded in a perfect square. 'I guess our souls are made of different stuff.'

Just then, a car beeps outside, and my tour of Fab's soul is over.

Downstairs, I insist that Fab stays inside even though he wants to come out to the car with me.

'No way,' I say, knowing what a fuss Mum will make if I introduce her to Fab, a boy she's never met before. 'I can get in a car on my own.'

'In that case, I will put the finishing touches to the collage.'

'Don't you dare add any pink to my side!'

True to his word, Fab stays in the house.

'So who lives in there?' asks Mum, the second I get in the car.

'A man of mystery!' I say as mysteriously as possible, and then I'm bombarded with questions for the whole journey home.

FIFTEEN

or the rest of the week, Fab claims to be improving our collage and when we hand it in on Friday, Miss Caudle clasps her hands to her chest and declares it's perfect. Then she sticks it in the centre of her display board, making Romilly announce that, just as she suspected, 'Fannie are Miss's favourites'.

'We do make an excellent team,' agrees Fab, as we gaze proudly at our poster.

Miss gets us to act out scenes from *Wuthering Heights*, which is fun, but I'm still pleased when we get to the end of the lesson because I'm hit with a rush of Friday Feeling. It's extra big because tomorrow is Sophie's party, and it looks like Jim was right: everyone's going.

As usual, Fab and I are the last to leave the room.

'Goodbye, Miss Cuddle,' says Fab. 'I hope you have an enjoyable weekend.'

'Urrgh,' she says, dropping a pile of folders into a box. 'Hardly. Marking and mowing my lawn. I've got a massive garden and a push lawnmower. It'll take me ages, but it's got to be done.'

'I will come and do it for you,' says Fab, without missing a beat. 'We have an excellent electric lawnmower. What is your address?'

Miss Caudle's eyes shoot open. 'Oh no, I couldn't ask you to do that, Fab.'

'Yes.' He whips his notebook out of his bag. 'I insist.'

An awkward moment follows as a range of emotions flash across Miss Caudle's face: amusement, shock, horror … temptation.

I decide to help her out. 'Fab, you can't just go round to a teacher's house and mow their lawn.'

'Why not? Miss Cuddle's grass is long: I can cut it.'

'Because it breaks some sort of teacher law, right, Miss?'

Miss Caudle nods. 'It wouldn't be professional of me to invite a student to my home.'

'Why wouldn't it be professional?'

'Look, Fab,' I say, 'a teacher can't encourage their sixteen-year-old students to come round to their garden to get all hot and sweaty.'

Fab's eyes widen in horror as he realises what I'm

hinting at. 'But I just want to help! Miss Cuddle, is your lawn very untidy and are you very busy?'

She sighs deeply. 'Yes and yes, but I'm afraid Annie's right.'

'Then I will come on Saturday and bring my mother. She will be my ... what do you call it? In Poland it is *przyzwoitka*.'

I get out my phone. 'Spell it,' I say. A moment later, I tell Miss Caudle, 'Fab's mother's going to be his chaperone.'

A smile spreads over her face. 'Well, if your mum's there, I'm sure there won't be a problem. I'd love to meet her!'

'And she would love to meet you. We will bring cake, *szarlotka*. It's very nice – apple cake with crumble on the top.'

'No, if you're mowing my lawn then the least I can do is provide the cake.'

'We'll see,' says Fab. He is so bringing cake.

After he's got Miss Caudle's address, we walk down the corridor together.

'Fab,' I say, when I get to my form room, 'is there anything you *think* of saying but choose not to because of, I don't know, peer pressure ... etiquette ... embarrassment?'

Fab considers my question carefully. 'Never,' he says. 'Life is too short for embarrassment.'

'Yeah, I used to think that too,' I say, 'before I met you.'

And this makes Fab drop one of his Incredible Hulk arms round my shoulders and laugh so hard that he almost knocks me over.

SIXTEEN

*P*AR-TAAAAAAY!* is not what I think when I wake up on Saturday morning. I'm a bit more: *urrgh, party ... really?*

I lie in bed, my entire body aching from three whole weeks of commuting to college. For a moment, I consider ringing Hilary and cancelling tonight, but then I remind myself that I'm her friend, and friends make sacrifices for each other. Even if we only go to the party for a bit, that's better than nothing. Plus, I'm starting to get to know everyone at college and I'd quite like to be seen as a party animal, even if right now I feel more like a party insect – an ant, say, or a woodlouse.

I've got a whole day to recover. I just need to chill out and get some energy back.

I pick up my phone and ring Mum's number. She answers straight away.

'Good morning, favourite daughter,' she says.

'Where are you?'

I hear her take a sip of tea. 'In the kitchen. You know I'm in the kitchen – that's why you're ringing.'

I laugh. 'True. So, please will you make me some toast?'

'Butter and Marmite?'

'And maybe a hot chocolate?'

'You're pushing your luck, but, OK, just this once.'

'Thanks, Mum. The room service here is excellent.'

'I wouldn't know. I've never tried it.'

'Mate, it's not my fault I can't carry a tray upstairs … So insensitive.'

'Ha, ha. See you in five minutes.'

I pull open the curtains, pile up some pillows on my bed and pick up *Wuthering Heights*. Heathcliff has just brought his wife, Isabella, home and I've got a feeling things aren't going to go too well: Isabella's called Heathcliff a monster and he's said he'd like to crush out her entrails. I've finally encountered a couple who get on worse than my mum and dad. Just.

I roll out of bed around midday, meet up with a friend from secondary school for ice cream, then do a lazy workout at the gym with my personal trainer, Sabine. That's right, like Kim Kardashian and Jay-Z, I have a personal trainer. Sabine is a university student who's doing a PhD on disability in sport and because I'm her guinea pig I get the sessions for free. Today I tell her I need to save my energy so we just do a bit of stretching and a lot of talking about her holiday in Thailand.

I spend the rest of the day lounging in my room, reading and letting my mind run over the past few weeks at Cliffe – and stalking my new friends online.

Personally, I'm not that into social media. I'm not on Snapchat or Instagram, and the last time I posted on Facebook was four weeks ago (a picture of Alice eating a grape). I suppose I like to keep things to myself rather than share them online, but, luckily for me, my new friends don't feel the same way.

Jim's clearly a fan of obscure music and comedy and TV, which I already knew, and Hilary seems dedicated to sharing inspirational quotes with the world: 'Everyone is gifted, but some people never open their package!' It turns out she's not following her own advice because, buried away, I discover a film of her cousin playing the guitar and Hilary singing along to a country song called 'Getting Ready to Get Down'. She kept that quiet, although now I think of it, she does seem very fond of a certain pair of cowboy boots.

I can't see Mal's Facebook page as he hasn't accepted

my friend request … Tonight I'm going to have to crush out his entrails.

Unexpectedly, it's Oliver's online presence which really captures my imagination. He's reposted loads of pest-related articles which are basically Annie clickbait: 'Zombie cockroaches are real and this wasp controls them!', 'Bug of the month!' and, my personal favourite, 'Today is Race Your Mouse Day!'

Fab is on Facebook but his page doesn't offer up many clues as most of it's written in Polish. I'm just considering opening up Google Translate when I realise how late it is. Hilary will be round soon and I need to make my bedroom ready to receive guests.

When she rings the doorbell half an hour later, I've picked up all my clothes, cleaned out the rats and even blown up the airbed. *This is good*, I think, as I look round my unusually tidy room. A bit cramped, but essentially good.

Downstairs, I can hear Mum chatting to Hilary, all excited that I've finally invited a friend over.

'I'm up here!' I shout out, then I make a grab for my laptop.

When Hilary walks into my bedroom, I'm dancing around the room to Josh Ritter singing 'Getting Ready to Get Down'.

She stands in the doorway, watching me through narrowed eyes.

'Are you ready to get down, Hilary?' I shout over the music. 'Why didn't you tell me you're such an amazing singer?'

She grins and shrugs, then throws down her bag and joins me on the rug, singing along at the top of her voice.

I always thought my room was small, but here I am, dancing round it with a friend, and there's still room for the rats' cage and an airbed. I get this little shiver down my spine. Could Hilary's voice be awakening my inner party animal? I turn the music up a bit louder so that this rush of energy will carry me through the next few hours.

SEVENTEEN

Two hours later, Mum drops Hilary and me off on the seafront. The sun's setting and there's this huge mackerel sky stretching to the horizon. At least, I think it's a mackerel sky: rows of rippling blue clouds lit by the last rays of sunshine. The sea is covered in choppy waves and as we walk towards the East Bay Hotel, the wind is so fierce I have to abandon my crutches and put my arm through Hilary's just to stay upright.

'Have fun!' Mum calls as she drives past, tooting her horn.

I watch her go with only a slight pang of regret that I'm missing out on our usual Saturday night film and curry routine. But would a massive party animal like me really want to stay in, eat biryani and watch *Ghostbusters: Answer the Call* (again)? I look at the grand entrance to the East Bay Hotel. The windows are glowing and music is thudding out from a distant room. Er, yes, right now she would – just a bit.

Like she can read my thoughts, Hilary pulls me across the road and together we squeeze through the revolving doors. We follow the music and laughter and find ourselves in a huge ballroom.

'It's just like *Cinderella*!' says Hilary.

I sort of know what she means. Chandeliers line the ceiling and blue velvet curtains sweep the floor. If the room didn't smell faintly of roast dinners, I'd be feeling pretty glam. There's a DJ in the corner pumping out Tinie Tempah, but with the exception of a little girl in a white party dress the dance floor's deserted.

Hilary's arm tightens on mine as we scan the room. The edges are packed with people who all seem to know each other and neither of us has a clue who the birthday girl is.

'Over there,' I say, nodding towards a corner table where Jim is waving enthusiastically. Mal and Oliver are waving too, only less enthusiastically, and with wide, slightly alarmed eyes.

Jim jumps up from the table, hugs us and tells us we're 'the most beautiful women in the entire world'.

'What have you been drinking?' I ask, laughing.

'Truth potion,' he says. 'I'm going to the bar. What d'you want?'

'A Coke,' I say.

'A *Coke*? Sure you don't want anything else in that Coke?'

'No, thanks. If I drink alcohol I fall over.'

'Can I have an orange juice, please,' says Hilary, pulling some money out of her purse.

'Seriously?' says Jim. 'You want me to go up to the bar and order a Coke and an orange juice? Why don't you go wild and get a cup of tea while you're at it?'

'Actually, I'd love a cup of tea,' I say, 'and a real man would happily go and get me one.'

'Well, you picked the wrong people to hang out with,' says Mal, 'because we're not real men and Jim's barely a real boy.'

'Oh really?' Jim says. 'Then watch this.'

Five minutes later, he comes back with a tray. 'One Coke and one orange juice,' he says, putting them down on the table, 'and five cups of tea.'

We all raise our teacups to the moment Jim became a man.

For the next hour, the DJ desperately works through various dance hits in an attempt to get someone, anyone, up on the dance floor (the little girl's collapsed on her mum's lap). As we sit around, talking and listening to music, something pretty good happens. All my tiredness and aches and pains seem to drift away. Maybe it's the velvet curtains, or maybe it's the easy-going banter the boys are supplying … or just possibly it's the Panadol Extra that I took before I came out. Who knows? All that matters is that I'm really starting to love this party.

We talk to loads of people from college, Oliver gets more drinks and brings back a plate overflowing with crisps, cold pizza, and cheese and pineapple on sticks. At one point, Hilary and Oliver go off to the toilets together, which would be weird if it were anyone except Hilary and Oliver.

'Will you introduce me to the birthday girl?' I ask Jim, shouting to be heard over the music. 'It seems rude not to say hello.'

He leads me through the crowd to a girl wearing a big floaty dress and an even bigger smile.

It turns out Sophie is a bit excitable and uber-friendly, and instantly she's hugging me and telling me she adores my skirt and that I've got hair like Kim Kardashian. But then she kind of blows it by saying: 'You're the disabled girl from college, right? So what's wrong with you?'

Sophie and I are standing facing each other, her hands resting on my shoulders.

'Nothing's wrong with me,' I say. 'What's wrong with you?' This is my stock response to the old 'What's wrong with you?' question, and, to be honest, it can go one of two ways: badly or awkwardly. Tonight, it goes a third way.

Sophie throws her head back, cackles and bellows, 'I'm allergic to strawberries!' Then she turns to Jim and says, 'And you're the guy who looks like the ugly one from One Direction, but, you know, in a good way because you're normal and he's gorgeous.' Then she releases me and wanders off towards the toilets. 'Thanks for coming,' she calls over her shoulder.

'Man, that was harsh,' says Jim, as we walk back to our table.

'I think you should take the 1D thing as a badly phrased compliment,' I tell him. We weave through the people hovering around the edge of the dance floor. 'It's like saying that out of Harry Potter, Ron and Hermione, your magic is as good as Ron's. Yes, he's the worst at magic, but he's still tons better at magic than most people.'

'Yeah,' he says, smiling. 'You're right. Cheers, Annie!' Then he throws an arm over my shoulder and gives me a sweaty hug.

EIGHTEEN

S alt 'n' Pepa's 'Push It' is what finally gets everyone dancing. I'm not sure if Sophie's mum requested it, but she is instantly up and owning that dance floor. And that's all it takes to make everyone who's been hovering start to dance. I'm sitting with Hilary, eating birthday cake, when James Brown's 'Sex Machine' comes on.

'I love this song,' she says, and starts singing along.

Then we notice that the dancing seems to have stopped and that something is happening. More and more people are getting to their feet and crowding around the dance floor. Hilary stands on her tiptoes.

'What's going on?' I ask.

'It think it's some sort of dance-off,' she says. 'Yep, some boys are doing a dance-off. I saw the vibe being passed, you know, like this.' She points at me and kind of waves her arm like an octopus.

'Are you sure?' I get up and join her at the edge of the clapping circle. 'I thought dance-offs only happened in films.'

She shrugs. 'Want to watch?'

'Do I?' I say, and we push our way to the front.

And there, right in the middle of the dance floor, throwing all six feet something of his body around with wild abandon, is Fab.

Am I surprised to discover Fab breakdancing at the centre of this clapping crowd? Not a bit. He seems very at home. He's wearing one of his loosely buttoned shirts and showing too much chest, but then so am I, so I can't really criticise. He's also wearing an old man's flat cap, back to front, which I'm fairly certain I last saw on Sophie's grandad.

Along with everyone else, Hilary and I cheer Fab on. The fact that he can't actually breakdance isn't putting him off. He drops down to the ground, spins on his shoulders and then sort of *humps* his way backwards across the empty space, banging his fists together at the same time. Which is how he ends up by my feet.

'Annie!' He reaches for an upside-down high five, then pops up – actually, he does this pretty well – and shouts, 'I gave Miss Cuddle's lawn stripes!' He pulls his flat cap round the right way, spins on his toes à la Michael Jackson and points randomly into the crowd, and the person he points at is Mal.

For a second, my heart goes out to quiet Mal, but I don't need to worry because, unlike Fab, Mal can *actually* break-dance – or at least he knows three moves, which is enough to get everyone generously whooping at his efforts. After a couple of quick backspins, he passes the vibe on to Jim.

Jim makes a big show of getting the crowd going, strutting round the circle clapping his hands over his head, before dropping to the floor and doing a totally lame windmill. He looks like he's fallen over and can't get up – like a turtle on its back – but no one cares. He scrambles to his feet and his eyes flick round the circle as he looks for the next victim.

His eyes fall on me and linger, but then he turns and points at Hilary.

She groans and her hand finds mine. I know exactly why Jim chose her and not me. He wanted to save me from an awkward situation because I wouldn't want to dance in front of everyone, would I? I mean, I can't even walk 'properly', so how could I ever dare to dance in the centre of a clapping circle?

Since the day I was born, I've been hit with moments like this, when people decide what I can and can't do. Most moments of ableism I choose to ignore – actually, loads, because I have to live my life – but every now and then, I think, damn it, I need to teach you guys a lesson.

And now is one of those moments.

The claps are losing their momentum and people are jostling Hilary, pushing her forward. No one wants this impromptu dance battle to end.

Suddenly, the DJ blends 'Sex Machine' into Beyoncé's 'Crazy in Love'.

I let go of Hilary's hand. 'I'll dance for you,' I say, then I walk straight into the middle of the empty dance floor.

'Crazy in Love' is totally MY song.

All around me, expressions of delight are frozen in place as people try to show how cool they are with this situation, but one girl gasps and puts a hand up to her mouth with horror. I lift my head a little higher. There's no going back now. Then I fix my eyes on the gasper, put my arms above my head and start to dance. I dance just like I do at home, like everyone should: like I'm happy and free, and loving my body and loving the music.

'Yeah!' Fab's deep voice cuts above the claps. 'Shake that *ass*, Annie!'

I'm definitely shakin' my ass. It's my signature move.

Fab's words seem to release something in the room because then everyone joins in, shouting, clapping and telling me I'm killing it.

Sophie's mum calls out, 'You're better than Beyoncé, darling!', which is so clearly rubbish I burst out laughing.

I do some on-the-spot robot dancing to give my legs a break, then turn round and point at Sophie. The birthday girl doesn't need to be asked twice. She runs towards me, skids on a grape and hits the ground like a ton of drunk bricks.

And so ends the epic dance battle …

I think I won!

NINETEEN

know it's time to go home when the DJ puts on James Blunt's 'You're Beautiful'.

I watch from my seat as the dance floor clears in seconds, leaving a handful of couples shuffling in circles and either trying to avoid touching or making sure their entire bodies are glued together.

After I've called Mum, I go to find Hilary, who disappeared ages ago in search of birthday cake. That's when Fab suddenly appears in front of me. He does one of his bows and holds out his hand.

'Oh no,' I say, laughing, because I know what's coming next.

'Dance with me, Annie,' he says, and I swear he almost goes down on one knee.

I shake my head. 'Sorry, Fab, but I'm a solo dancer. Dancing with someone else would ruin my moves.' This

103

is only partly true. The couples dancing do look a bit dorky, but who cares? Actually, it's the intensity I'd hate: standing face-to-face with someone, trapped in their arms, with nowhere to look except into their eyes. I suppress a shudder at the thought.

'But you have never danced with *me*,' Fab says, patting his chest. 'How do you know *I* would ruin your moves?'

'Sorry,' I say firmly, 'but slow dancing's not my thing.'

After a moment, he shrugs. 'I understand. It's not really my thing either.'

'So why did you ask me?'

'You will only know if you dance with me,' he says.

'Looks like I'm never going to know then,' I say with a smile, then I head towards Hilary, who I've spotted back at our table.

'You will regret it!' he calls after me.

'Maybe,' I shout back, 'but at least I won't be slow dancing.'

'What was that all about?' asks Hilary.

'Just Fab being Fab-ish,' I say, and she nods as if I've made perfect sense.

Twenty minutes later, Hilary and I are outside the hotel, waiting for Mum to pick us up. Hilary's full of beans and has climbed on to the back of one of the stone lions that flank the doors to the hotel. 'Take me to the moon!' she yells, throwing back her head and slapping the lion's bottom. The sequins on her top glitter in the orange street lights.

I sit on a low wall, leaning against a pillar. It would be fair to say that I'm experiencing a colossal amount of leg ache right now, but nothing a hot chocolate and eight hours' sleep won't sort out.

'Annie!' Fab bounces down the stairs towards me. 'We didn't say goodbye.'

'Oh, sorry, Fab. Bye.' I give him a wave.

He smiles, but he doesn't go anywhere. Instead, he sits next to me, stares out to sea and starts drumming his hands on his legs. Then he turns to me and says, 'So, I have something to ask you. I was going to do it when we were dancing, but then you didn't want to dance and I lost my courage. But when I saw you sitting on this wall, I thought, it is a sign.'

I laugh. 'Sorry, you've lost me.'

He takes a deep breath and says, 'Annie Demos, will you be my girl?'

'*Your girl?*' I look at him, smiling and frowning at the same time. My ears are still ringing from the music and my mind is buzzing from talking to so many people. 'Fab, I don't get it.'

'In Poland, we don't say "girlfriend" or "boyfriend".

We say "my girl", *moja dziewczyna*, or "my boy", *mój chłopak*. So, Annie, I am asking you: will you be *moja dziewczyna*?'

'He's asking you out!' Hilary yells from her lion.

'Exactly!' Fab takes my hand. 'Annie, will you be my girl and go on a date with me?'

I'm so surprised that I nearly burst out laughing. 'Are you joking, Fab? Because it's really hard to tell right now.'

He shakes his head. 'Annie, you know I wouldn't joke about this.'

I sit up a bit taller. 'No, right, sorry. It's just … I didn't see that coming.' And it's true – I didn't – although, now I think about it, from the moment I met Fab he's been very into me. But I didn't think I was getting special treatment: he's very into everything.

'So, what's your answer?' His voice is quieter now.

Behind him, I see Hilary looking at me with big eyes and barely concealed excitement. I look away quickly before she makes me laugh.

'I'm sorry, but my answer is no,' I say, giving his hand a squeeze then letting go. 'But thank you for asking me. I mean, you're great and everything, Fab, but I'm not interested in being anyone's girl. I don't want to be anyone's anything! I just want to hang out with my friends and have fun.'

'But, Annie, you can have fun with me. We are perfect for each other. Everyone can see it: we're Fannie!'

I laugh and shift a little bit away from him. 'That's just a silly name Romilly's given us because we sit next to each other and talk a lot. It doesn't mean anything.'

'I think you are wrong. It does mean something. I knew you would become *moja dziewczyna* the moment I walked into the English room and our eyes met.'

Now I do laugh. 'Fab, our eyes only met because everyone else looked the other way. You don't believe in all that stuff, do you?'

'What stuff?'

'Fate bringing two people together … Eyes meeting across a crowded room … It was written in the stars … "*I am Heathcliff!*"'

He smiles. 'Of course. Don't you? Without love, life is pointless.'

'Life *is* pretty pointless,' I say, 'but human beings are good at inventing meaning.'

'No, no.' He shakes his head. 'If love is an invention, then why do people feel incredible when they fall in love? If you feel it –' he thumps his fist against his chest '– then it is real.'

'No, my friend told me about this. When we're drawn to someone, our brains think, danger, and go into fight-or-flee mode, flooding our bodies with cortisol. The cortisol makes our hearts pound and everything feel hyper-intense. Basically, being "in love" is the same as being really scared, which should tell you something, but human beings have just put a romantic gloss on it.'

Hilary has flopped forward on the lion and is listening to our conversation with interest. 'But even animals love each other,' she says. 'I watched this documentary where this polar bear nearly starved to death just to keep her cub alive.'

Great. Now she's joining in! 'That's the instinct to survive,' I say.

Fab frowns. 'So you really think love –'

'– is a fairytale, a narrative we've spun around our basic animal instinct to keep the human race going.'

'And I am asking you out because?'

'You're programmed to do it.' I tap my head. 'Even though it's illogical and will lead to heartbreak.'

Fab puffs his cheeks out and sighs. 'That is depressing, Annie.'

I shrug. 'No, it's realistic.'

'So what's the point of life then?'

'I've already told you: to have fun, to have an adventure!'

Fab's eyes light up. 'And I've already told you: there is no greater adventure in life than love.'

108

I laugh. 'Really? Well, I'll travel the world – visit Machu Picchu, snorkel the Great Barrier Reef, see the Northern Lights – and you can go on a load of dates, and in ten years' time we'll meet up and see who's had the best adventure.'

'So, you're saying you *won't* go out with me?'

'No, I won't. But thank you for asking me.'

For a moment he looks crestfallen, then he brightens up. 'Maybe we can go out as friends until you change your mind.'

A small part of me wants to say 'yes': I'd enjoy hanging out with Fab – he's funny and unpredictable and I love the way he argues with me – but I could never be the girlfriend he would want. He'd want dates and devotion. He'd want to hold hands. I hate holding hands with people. It makes me want to scream! I can hear the sea crashing on the beach and a cool wind is blowing into my face, but right now, sitting next to Fab, I feel hot and uncomfortable.

'We'll see each other at college,' I say, looking out for Mum's car.

He studies me a little longer, then shrugs and smiles. 'OK, no worries.' Despite his height and his confidence and his bare arms where he's rolled up his sleeves, Fab suddenly seems like a little boy. 'I'll see you at college,' he says, then he stands up and walks back up the steps and into the hotel.

I turn to Hilary. 'Did I just imagine that?'

'Nope,' she says, hugging the lion. 'Fab asked you to be his girl. You said, "No, thanks." So, essentially, nothing's changed.'

She's right. Nothing's actually changed ... And yet, I can't shake the feeling that in the past few minutes everything has changed.

TWENTY

Somehow, Hilary manages to keep quiet about the whole Fab thing all the way home in the car.

'What's up with you two?' asks Mum. 'You're very subdued. Didn't you have a good time?'

'It was great,' I say in my cheeriest voice. 'Wasn't it, Hilary?' I turn round and give her a look, a look that says, *Speak!*

'It was brilliant,' she bursts out. 'Loads of dancing, cake, crisps. It was brilliant! Especially the crisps.'

I give her another look, a look that says, OK, *stop speaking!*

'Well, I'm glad you girls had fun. You're going to have lots to talk about tonight.'

'Oh, we will,' says Hilary, leaning forward so that her head pokes through the gap between the seats. 'Won't we, Annie?'

111

* * *

An hour later, Hilary and I are lying on my bed eating curry toasties.

It's amazing how quickly I've got used to having Hilary around. I did have a moment of wishing she wasn't here when Alice and Mabel ran on to her lap and made a big fuss of her, but then I reminded myself that friends share their favourite things, and that includes their rats.

'This is the best,' says Hilary, holding up her toastie. 'I can't believe I've never thought of putting curry in between two pieces of buttered bread and frying the whole thing.' Her eyes slide towards me. 'Sooo, a few weeks at college and already someone's asked you out.'

'I know. I didn't realise I was so desirable. No, that's not true. Obviously, I know I'm gorgeous, but *Fab*? And, *bam*, "Will you be my girl?" Just like that!'

'He obviously doesn't believe in taking things slow.' She nibbles her toastie. 'So do you really not want to go out with anyone, or were you using that as an excuse to let him down gently?'

I think about the couples I knew at school. 'The thing is, I know loads of people who've changed after they started going out with someone. They become all boyring.'

Hilary laughs. 'But *you* wouldn't have to become boyring.'

'Oh, everyone says that, but they always change in the end. They wear black because the object of their desire wears black, or they become a vegetarian overnight even though they've been declaring love for bacon sandwiches for years.'

'But that could be good, couldn't it?' says Hilary. 'For pigs at least.'

I laugh, flop back on the bed and stretch out. 'Maybe, but I guess I don't think it's worth the hassle. Urrgh, and the fights!'

'You're not selling it to me,' says Hilary, looking disappointed. 'I've never even kissed anyone, but I was kind of looking forward to it all.'

'I'm into *kissing*. It's the you're-my-girlfriend-now-never-speak-to-another-person part that I'm not into.'

'So if Fab had asked for a kiss?'

I consider this for a moment, then shake my head. 'No way. You could never just kiss Fabian Kaczka then go back to being friends the next day. You heard him. He practically proposed to me back there! Look, I'll be totally honest with you, Hilary. You're the first person I've invited round to my house in years. I like my own time and my own space too much. I *need* it. I suppose I'm protective of it.'

She sits up a little taller and smiles. 'I'm honoured! What made you ask me?'

I look at her and smile. 'Well, you're pretty undemanding.' This is true. Hilary never seems bothered if I tell her I have to work during lunchtimes or break. (She just says, 'OK. See you later, alligator,' and floats off somewhere.) 'Also, I realised you were worth losing a bit of my freedom for.'

'Unlike Fab?'

The way she says this makes me feel bad for him. 'No, he is a great person – like you – but he would be seriously high maintenance.'

'Like a vintage Aston Martin?'

I laugh. 'I guess so.'

'Whereas I'm more of a Beetle.'

'Or a yellow Mini.'

She smiles, obviously liking the sound of that. Then her smile switches to a frown. 'Poor Fab!' she says.

'Not poor Fab. Lucky Fab, because I would drive him mad. Tonight, I saved him from a miserable experience.'

'He didn't look too pleased about it.'

I think about Fab's face just before he walked back into the hotel. 'No, but one day he'll thank me.'

'I love his chest,' Hilary says dreamily. 'It's ultra manly.' Then she makes this long, drawn-out *mmmmm*, similar to the one she did when she bit into her toastie.

I curl up on my side. 'That chest comes with conditions, Hilary.'

'You think he's got the message?'

'*Definitely*.'

TWENTY-ONE

On Monday, I discover that Fab has not, in fact, got the message.

I'm sitting in the common room, chatting to Oliver and Hilary, when Kate Bush's 'Wuthering Heights' comes on. Piano music sweeps across the room and I start swaying along as Kate Bush breathily whoops and sings about Heathcliff and being 'so cold'.

Then I notice Fab dancing his way towards us, singing the words at the top of his voice.

'Oh, God,' I say, shrinking behind Hilary.

Despite the fact that I'm obviously trying to hide from him, Fab carries on pointing at me and doing his wavy-armed dance and singing until the track ends and he says, 'Annie, that was *our* song. Let's celebrate our song being played in the common room by going on a date!'

I narrow my eyes and shake my head. 'Fab, we don't have a song.'

'We do. That was it.'

'Sorry. "Wuthering Heights" may be an awesome power ballad but the answer's still "no".'

'For today,' he says with a mysterious smile. Then he wanders over to the coffee shop to flirt with Peggy.

'*Ahhh*,' says Hilary.

'No, Hilary, not *ahhh*. More *urrgh*. Fab's stalking me.'

'He's wooing you!'

'Is there a difference?' I say.

On Tuesday, Miss Caudle gets us all to set up Twitter accounts and form a *Wuthering Heights* study group. When we're supposed to be writing succinct definitions of the Gothic, Fab sends me a GIF of a tap-dancing fox with the words *umówisz sie ze mna* shaved into its fur.

Google Translate tells me I've been asked out again, so I reply with a GIF of a parrot shaking its head.

'Stop mucking around, you two!' calls Miss Caudle from the front of the room, and that's when I realise Fab included our study group's hashtag when he sent me the fox.

Five minutes later, I discover Miss has also been on Google Translate because when I look up, I catch her smiling at us fondly.

I narrow my eyes and shake my head.

'Sorry,' she mouths.

On Wednesday, I get a message tucked under my waffle (he must have got Peggy to help him with that one).

On Thursday, it's a simple Post-it note stuck to my wheelchair with *Annie + Fab* = randka? written on it. *Randka*, I discover, means 'date'.

I tell Hilary about the Post-it note during lunchtime on Friday.

'Bit creepy?' she asks.

'No, I've started to enjoy being asked out on a daily basis,' I say, and it's true – I have. I like working out how Fab's going to pop the question, plus he's asking me in such silly ways that I don't feel any of the panic I felt on the night of Sophie's party. It's almost become a game and I guess he's doing this to prove to me that going out with him would be fun. 'But he hasn't asked me out today and he's already spoken to me three times.'

'Maybe he's saving it up for the barbecue.'

The barbecue's happening after college to raise money for Amnesty International.

I shake my head. 'I don't think so.'

Hilary sighs. 'Maybe you're right. Maybe he's given

up.' She sips her coffee sadly. 'Man, I hope he hasn't. You guys are my OTP.'

'Your *what*?'

'My One True Pairing.'

I laugh. 'Well, sorry to ruin your ludicrous romantic fantasy, but I think he's finally got the message.'

As soon as the words are out of my mouth, I realise that, like Hilary, I'm feeling disappointed too, which is odd because I really should be feeling relieved. The thing is, Fab's relentless attention might be a bit embarrassing, but it's still flattering.

I gulp my coffee down, knowing it will cheer me up. This week Hilary and I have got very into our coffee, having a couple every break and lunchtime. I need to cut back. Last night my mind was buzzing so much that I found myself cleaning out Alice and Mabel at midnight, singing along with Kate Bush to 'Wuthering Heights'. Since Fab played it in the common room, I've had it on constantly. Not that I'm telling Fab that.

All the way through English, I can't help being on tenterhooks, looking out for a message or note from Fab. At one point, while we're reading in silence, he nudges me and slides his notebook towards me, and I feel my heart speed up and a tingle of anticipation.

What is 'disquietude'? he's written.

Feeling anxious, I write back, my heart returning to its normal speed.

At the end of the lesson, when we're packing up our bags, and Fab still hasn't asked me out, I realise it's time for me to accept that my week of Fab attention is over. He's finally given up on me.

I feel tiredness wash over me and I'm grateful I've brought my wheelchair to the lesson. I wonder if the cafe is still open. Despite my good intentions, I suddenly have an overwhelming desire for a cappuccino.

'Annie!' Fab calls as I release the brakes.

I turn round. 'Yes, Fab?'

'Can you take these sausages down to the field?'

He passes me a bulging plastic bag. 'Er, why?'

'For the barbecue.'

Perfect. Instead of a quirky request for a date, I'm holding a bag of dead pig. For a vegetarian, this is a double blow.

'Did you forget?' he asks, thinking my look of disappointment is one of confusion.

'No, I was just thinking of popping to the coffee shop, but I can take the sausages down.' I'm slightly cheered by the fact that Fab's asked me to help him. So often people's eyes skip over me when they need a favour. Although this is a particularly gross favour. The bag is heavy in my lap.

The meat feels cold and, well, a bit fleshy through the thin plastic.

'Let's go to the coffee shop together,' he says, picking up a cardboard box. 'We can get to the field that way.'

'Great!' I fix a smile on my face and follow him out of the room.

For me, the barbecue turns out to be one burnt vegetarian sausage, something fizzy and blue, and a heck of a lot of crisps, but it's fun lounging around on the field with everyone else from our year. Faces and names are becoming more familiar and there's this relaxed vibe that only gets better as the afternoon fades into early evening, and more and more people turn up. Even when the food's finished no one wants to go home. Speakers send music drifting across the field and it's one of those late summer evenings, when the sky is perfectly blue and it's still too warm for coats.

I'm sitting with Hilary and the boys on the grass when Fab comes over. 'So, guys,' he says, slapping his hands together. 'There's a rounders game taking place. Who's playing?'

Jim's eyes dart in my direction. Since the party last Saturday, I've had the feeling he's being extra careful with me. I haven't got a clue if he remembers passing me over in the dance-off, but there's been something slightly over the top about the way he's talked to me, like he's desperate to prove he doesn't care or even notice that I'm disabled. 'Yeah,' he says. 'We'll play, right?'

'Why not?' I say.

'Great!' says Fab, giving Jim a matey pat on the back that nearly knocks his drink out of his hand.

Then Fab goes to find more players, Hilary goes to find more coffee and we take up our positions on the rounders pitch.

When Hilary gets back, I ask her to be backstop with me. Partly, this is so I have someone to get rid of all my excess chat with, but I also want her to do the running for me. Catching and throwing I'm OK at – running not so much.

It's the most relaxed rounders game ever. No one keeps track of the score, people who should be out stay in, and the teams are constantly changing. Hilary and I chat or taunt whoever's batting depending on how well we know them, and Fab runs around keeping everyone motivated and declaring things are 'amazing' far too often.

Before long it's his turn to bat.

'You two can sit down because this ball is going to fly,' he says, squinting into the distance. 'It might reach Poland.'

'Or it might land in my hands,' I say. 'Get ready, Hilary. I've got a powerful feeling Fab's going to miss this.'

'Hello, ice-cream van …' says Hilary, drifting away from us.

'Hilary! Get back here!'

But she just mutters something about needing a ninety-nine and keeps walking across the field. If caffeine makes me loud and chatty, it makes Hilary quiet and dizzy.

Fab does a few trial swings with the bat. 'Seriously, Annie. Go with Hilary. Take it easy. I'm extremely good at this sport.'

'Fab, what sport are we playing?'

He thinks for a moment. 'Circles?'

I laugh. 'Would I be right in thinking this is the first time you've ever played rounders?'

He shrugs. 'You would, but it seems the same as baseball and I've played that.'

Ahead of us, the bowler tosses the ball up and down, waiting for us to stop talking.

'OK. Here goes.' Fab blows twice into his cupped hand. 'Come on, Fabian, *pokaż im*!'

Then he crouches down low, as the bowler jogs forward and sends the ball flying towards us. I cup my hands, Fab swings the bat and then there's a mighty *thwack* as the ball soars into the air.

Fab punches his fist in the air. 'AMAZING!'

But instead of legging it to the first post, he turns and faces me. 'Go out with me, Annie.' He thumps his chest with the bat. 'Just once. Look how I hit balls!'

And I'm so happy that he's asked me out just when I've given up on him, and so much caffeine is spinning through my bloodstream, that I ignore the voice of reason that's hidden inside me shouting, *No, Annie. No, NO!* Instead I laugh and say, 'OK, why not?'

'*Tak!*' says Fab, then he throws down the bat and runs round the entire pitch, roaring and high-fiving every fielder he meets. He slides into the final post a fraction of a second before the ball makes contact.

And the crowd goes wild.

'Got you an ice cream,' says Hilary, thrusting the cone under my nose. 'What's going on?'

'Fab scored a rounder.'

'Huh,' she says, nibbling the Flake sticking out of her ice cream.

'And I agreed to go out with him.'

Hilary starts to laugh.

I scowl. 'It would never have happened if you hadn't *had* to get an ice cream.'

In the centre of the pitch, Fab's running around with his shirt pulled over his head and I can just make out Jackson chasing him, also with his shirt over his head. They both rugby-tackle Mal and knock him to the ground.

'They taste good though, right?' says Hilary.

I smile and take a lick of my ice cream. 'Very!'

124

TWENTY-TWO

My caffeine-fuelled good mood stays with me all the way to the station (I fly down that hill!), the whole journey home (I thrash Jackson at two-player *Tetris*!) and halfway into Friday evening (Mum's back early!).

But around the time Mum's dumping a pizza in front of me, niggling doubt has crept into my mind and I'm wondering what I've let myself in for.

'What's up with you?' asks Mum, sitting next to me on the sofa and putting on the TV.

'We've run out of ketchup,' I say.

No way am I telling her about the whole Fab date thing. She'd be way too excited. She's desperate for me to go out with someone. She says it's because 'first love is just the best', but I suspect she just wants concrete evidence that I'm not a loner. Having Hilary round has reassured her considerably, but a boyfriend really would be the ultimate proof for her.

So I keep quiet until I'm upstairs, then I message Hilary.

Regretting Fab date ...

Why? It'll be a laugh!!

Hmmmm ...

What does that mean?

I'm expressing my uncertainty about the whole date situation through a noise: hmmmm.

Mate, he hasn't asked you to MARRY him. It's a date! Relax! Woof!

He asked me on a date, which, from my POV, is the same as marriage. Who even asks people on dates these days?? No one, except Fab, the boy I've agreed to go on a date with! I feel like I've time-warped to the 1950s. Hang on ... Are you expressing encouragement via the sound 'woof'?

Woof woof! 🐾

Despite Hilary's woofs, all weekend I fail to relax.

Why have I agreed to do the one thing I specifically did not want to do? Every time I try to imagine the two of us on the date, I get this claustrophobic panicky feeling inside, like I'm in a hot room with too many people, and the radiators are on full blast, and I'm wearing a polo-neck jumper (made of polyester) with a vest *and* a T-shirt … and then someone hands me a cup of tea. A really hot cup of tea.

Basically, I feel trapped, and I haven't even been on the date yet.

It's such a bad feeling that on Monday morning when Fab sits next to me in English, I try to tell him I've changed my mind.

'Look, about this date, Fab –'

'I have it all planned out,' he says, pulling out his yellow notebook. 'What is your address? On Saturday, my uncle Emil will pick you up at two p.m.'

I use *Wuthering Heights* as a fan. 'Right, about that. Fab, this isn't a *date* date. You know that, right?'

Fab laughs. 'It's cool, Annie. Don't worry. We're just two friends who are going to pick blackberries. You're going to love it!'

'*Blackberries?*'

'Yes, the fruit that grows on bushes.'

'Fab, I know what blackberries are. It's just … not what I was expecting.'

He frowns. 'You don't want to go?'

I think for a moment. Actually, picking blackberries sounds fine. Fab's been going on about this date for so long that I assumed we'd be doing something embarrassingly intense and couply, like a eating in a restaurant with tablecloths and candles, or holding hands in the back row of the cinema.

'Blackberry-picking is fine,' I say, 'as long as you've thought through what I can do.'

'What can you do?'

'Well, I can walk, obviously, just not too far. And I get tired at the weekend.'

'It will be perfect,' he says. Just then, Miss Caudle walks into the room and Fab jumps to his feet. 'Miss Cuddle, I have your apples.' He pulls a paper bag out of his rucksack and puts it on her desk. 'And this Saturday, Annie and I will be picking blackberries so we will get some for you.'

'Oooh,' she says. 'Apple and blackberry crumble is my favourite.'

'You are welcome to come if you like,' says Fab, spreading his arms wide. 'My mother knows a top-secret spot that is full of blackberries.'

As Fab chats to Miss Caudle, I tune out. Now Fab has invited our teacher on our 'date' and the last hint of romance has vanished. This is good. Really good. Blackberry-picking doesn't feel like the start of something big; it just feels like hanging out with a friend. All the invisible pressure disappears and, when Fab sits back down, I realise I'm actually looking forward to going.

'She didn't want to come?' I ask.

Fab shrugs. 'She has a yoga workshop.'

'Have you thought of inviting the rest of the class? Or maybe Peggy?'

He thinks for a moment.

'Fab, that was a joke! You, me and your uncle Emil will be fine.'

'Ah,' he says. 'There might be one or two other members of my family there. You see, there are *a lot* of blackberries.'

TWENTY-THREE

I decide to leave telling Mum about my blackberry-picking date until the last possible moment. As in, the moment when a green van roars down our road, pulls up on the kerb and Fab and his uncle climb out.

Mum and I are in the front garden trying to fix the roof on the bird table when this happens.

'What the … ?' says Mum, as Fab clears the flower bed in one leap and strides towards us.

Fab does look quite alarming. He's wearing a black leather jacket over black shorts with flames licking around the hem, and it doesn't help that his uncle Emil is wearing a suit jacket with jeans and smoking a roll-up. It's all a bit rock and roll for our road.

Fab takes Mum's hand and gives it a hearty shake. 'It is very good to meet you, Mrs Demos!'

'It's Ms Mitchell, actually,' says Mum, then she turns to me, eyebrows raised expectantly.

'Mum,' I say, 'this is my friend Fab, from college, and this is his uncle Emil.' Uncle Emil nods and sucks on his cigarette. 'And we're all going blackberry-picking.'

'It is perfect weather, no?' says Uncle Emil, staring up at the blue sky.

'Yes, perfect,' says Mum, recovering quickly. It takes a lot to ruffle her feathers. 'Would you like a cup of tea? I'd love to hear a bit about you, Fab.' OK, she says this a bit pointedly and shoots me a look at the same time.

'I'm afraid we must get going, Ms Mitchell. We have to light a barbecue and make kebabs.' Fab pauses to tap the loose roof on the bird table. 'But first we will mend this little house.' Then he turns to Emil and delivers some instructions in Polish.

'You're Polish!' says Mum. 'Cześć!'

'Dzień dobry,' replies Fab.

'I've got three Polish students in my class and they've been teaching me all the important words,' says Mum.

Then, while she tries out her Polish on Fab, Emil attacks the bird table with a cordless drill. By the time I've gone into the house and got my coat, the bird table is fixed and Emil is loading his tools back into the van.

Fab drops his arm around my shoulder. He does this to

131

everyone at college, even Miss Caudle, but it still makes Mum raise her eyebrows.

'Well, have fun,' she says. 'Annie, don't you think you should take your wheelchair?'

I probably should – I don't know where we're going or how long I'm going to have to be on my feet – but the fact that she's thought of it and not me makes me shake my head.

'No. I'll be fine.'

Fab's eyes flick between us. 'We could take it in the van. Then, if you want it, Annie, you can say.'

'Fine,' I say, with a wave of my hand, and the wheelchair is brought out, folded and dutifully loaded into the back of Emil's van.

And then it's my turn to be loaded into the van. It's a big step up, but Fab and Mum know me well enough to leave me to it.

While I heave myself up and into the middle seat, Emil watches curiously.

'You need step,' he says. 'Next time, I bring step.' Then he drops his cigarette end in the gutter and climbs into the driver's seat.

Fab gets in next to me, and we're ready to go.

Mum stands on the kerb, arms folded, looking up at me squished between Fab and Emil.

132

'What?' I mouth, and this makes her laugh and shake her head.

'*Do widzenia*, Ms Mitchell,' says Fab, waving and leaning across me to toot Emil's horn.

Emil slaps his hand away.

'Bring me back some blackberries,' Mum calls.

It's great sitting in the van, all high up and bouncy. As we drive out of town, we listen to some sort of oompah band while Fab chats away, describing the delights that await me in the countryside. Although Uncle Emil doesn't speak English very well, this doesn't stop him interrupting whenever he thinks Fab's exaggerating.

'We have a very beautiful spot for the barbecue,' says Fab.

'Too much dog do-do,' Emil mutters darkly.

'And there are more blackberries than we'll be able to pick!'

'Many are small,' says Emil. 'And green.'

But Emil's more cynical approach doesn't put Fab off and his hands fly around as he describes his mother's perfect *szarlotka* and Aunt Dorota's famous *śmieciucha*.

It doesn't take me long to realise that I've been invited along to some sort of mega family outing, but this doesn't bother me. The more Fab describes how his *babcia*'s arthritis will stop her picking blackberries and how his cousin Patek is an annoying *idiota*, the less this feels like a date and I feel myself relaxing.

After twenty minutes, we pull in at a car park in a forest. A crowd of adults and children are gathered in one corner around a smoking barbecue. Deckchairs are arranged around it and an old lady is hunkered down in one of them. Fab's *babcia*, I'm guessing. Emil beeps his horn and everyone turns in our direction.

As Emil reverses the van into a space between two cars, Fab falls quiet and stares out of the window. It's as if he's only just considered the possibility that this might not be every teenager's idea of a good time.

'There is *a lot* of my family here. More than I realised,' he says, turning to look at me. 'Do you mind, Annie?'

'I'm half Greek, Fab,' I say with a shrug. 'This barely counts as a family gathering.'

He smiles in relief, then opens the van door. 'Well, I will look after you.' He stands and watches as I half fall out of the van.

'I don't need you to, but thanks all the same.'

Fab has obviously prepped his family about my cerebral palsy because everyone takes great care not to stare as I wobble my way across the car park. But still one little

134

girl can't take her eyes off me, until her mum pokes her in the back and then her eyes shoot down to the ground.

After Fab has introduced me to his mum – a tiny, quiet lady who really doesn't look like she could have produced a strapping giant like Fab – he grabs two empty plastic cartons and asks me if I can walk 'point seven five kilometres'.

'That's precise.'

He nods. 'I measured it on my phone the other day. The best blackberries and the best views are just over that hill.' He points towards a path that leads up through the woods.

'Point seven five kilometres,' I say. 'Yeah, I can definitely do that.'

Fab has an animated conversation with his mum in Polish, packs a few things in a bag, then we set off along the path.

'What was that about?'

'With my mother? She wanted me to feed you, but I said I would feed you on the hill.'

'Feed me what?'

'Cake.'

And then we fall quiet. Maybe it's the beautiful silence of the woods ... or maybe it's the birdsong ... or maybe it's the unfortunate image that has just popped into my head of Fab literally feeding me cake as I lie sprawled on some hill, but suddenly everything feels a bit … *intimate*.

'I love cake,' I say, to get things back on the right track. 'And chips.'

Fab looks at me out of the corner of his eye and smiles. 'Polish cake is the best,' he says.

We carry on up the path, then push through a bush (Fab goes first, like a battering ram) and burst out on a hillside.

'Wow …' I say, gazing out across the fields and rivers that stretch all the way to the sea.

'*Pieknie*,' says Fab.

'What's that?'

'Beautiful.'

'Come on,' I say, turning round to face the prickly bushes that line the edge of the hill. 'These blackberries won't pick themselves.'

This is the first time I've ever picked blackberries. For an infant teacher, my mum isn't that into nature and she's much more likely to take me for a walk along Brighton seafront than in the woods. As I pluck the berries off the branches and drop them into my tub, I wonder if this is because of me. Maybe Mum would like to do this, but focuses on smooth-surfaced museums and pavements to make my life easier.

Next to me, Fab whistles as he reaches the high-up berries. Summer's still clinging on, and it's so warm that after a while I take off my cardy so I can enjoy feeling the sun beating down on my arms. But I discover blackberry bushes are prickly and soon my arms are all scratched up.

'Here,' says Fab, passing me his leather jacket. 'This is why I'm wearing it. It stops the scratches.'

'No, thanks. I can handle it.'

He drops it next to my cardy. 'It's too hot anyway,' he says with a shrug, but then he's yelping and squealing every time a thorn catches his skin.

It turns out picking blackberries is very addictive. Just when I've cleared one branch of perfectly ripe fruit, I see more just a bit further along the hedgerow and I can't resist putting them in my tub too. The other thing I discover about blackberry-picking is that it's really easy to talk when you're facing a bush. Fab and I have never had any problem chatting, but with the addition of the bush, we're on fire.

He asks me about my dad, and I explain that my parents had the worst and shortest marriage ever.

'Now that they live two thousand miles apart they occasionally get on,' I say, then I tell him about the summers I've spent at my Greek nana – Yia Yia's – home in Karpathos and how I can't get an ice cream from

137

the shop without some old lady inviting me into her house and force-feeding me.

'Does she live in a village?' asks Fab.

'A tiny village called Lakia. Just a taverna, the shop and the sea.'

'And are the people in the village polite about your cerebral palsy?'

Even though I'm getting used to the way Fab says things so directly, his question surprises me – usually people do everything they can to avoid mentioning the fact that I'm disabled.

'*Polite* … ?' I say, thinking back to all my summers spent in Lakia. 'I'm not sure they're polite as in politically correct, but I've been visiting since I was a baby, so they're used to me … Plus Yia Yia is scary. Once a boy imitated my walk and she went out and whacked him with a fish.'

Fab looks alarmed. 'Is that a Greek thing to do?'

'No, it's a Yia Yia thing to do. She was that mad that she just went at him with what she had in her hands – a red mullet. Even my dad's scared of Yia Yia and he's a big man.' I glance over at Fab's blackberry tub and see that it's almost full. 'Hey, you're winning because I've been doing all the talking.' After a moment, I say, 'Tell me about your dad.' I've decided that it shouldn't just be Fab who gets to ask all the personal questions.

'My father lives in Poland. When my mother came to England I had to stay with him, but last year I joined my mother.'

Something about the way Fab says this, like he's choosing his words carefully, makes me think that there is something he's not telling me. 'So how long was your mum here without you?'

'Seven years, but she came back to Poland a lot, and I visited. That is how I learnt to speak English.'

I try to imagine Fab spending nearly half his childhood not living with his mum, that sweet lady who was pressing cake on us. I suppose it's no different from me and my dad, only for some reason it seems totally different.

'Do you miss him – your dad?'

Fab keeps picking his blackberries, and after a while, he says, 'Yes, but what I really miss is the three of us being together.'

I turn to look at him, waiting for him to continue.

'My happiest memories are from when my mother and father still lived together.'

'Maybe you will all live together again one day.'

He shakes his head. 'That will never happen.' Then he turns round and takes a deep breath in as he looks at the hill stretching in front of us. 'I want to run,' he says, then he puts his blackberries on the ground, smiles at me and goes running down the hill, roaring at the top of his voice, his long arms windmilling round.

He looks so free and happy that suddenly I want to join in, only I can't run like that, not downhill. So I decide to do something I haven't done for years. I lie down then start rolling down the hill. I come to a stop against a clump of grass and Fab runs back up to meet me.

'You are a crazy girl.' He drops a buttercup on my chest then lies down next to me.

'I'm a crazy girl who feels dizzy,' I say, taking the buttercup and holding it against the sun. 'Now, wasn't there talk of cake?'

TWENTY-FOUR

It turns out Fab's mum has put cake and some sort of cheese pasty into the rucksack.

'Let me get this straight,' I say, licking creamy icing off my fingers, 'this is some sort of pre-barbecue snack?'

He nods. 'And she has made you vegetarian sausages because the kebabs are made with lamb.'

'That's kind,' I say. And then, because the sun is shining and I'm full of cake and Fab's family are being so welcoming, I add, 'I'm glad I came.'

His face lights up. 'It's a good date?'

'Well, it's the only date I've ever been on so I've not got much to compare it to, but, yes. This is good, isn't it?'

Fab looks so pleased that I haven't got the heart to add my usual warning about us just being friends. I mentioned it so many times last week that I know he must have the message by now. Instead, we just sit on the hill and stare out at the endless sky and the view that surrounds us.

'Hey, Fab.' I turn to him. 'Have you ever done the Blue Experience?'

'No. It sounds unhappy.'

'It isn't. You lie down with your eyes shut for five minutes, then when you open your eyes everything looks blue.'

'Let's do it,' says Fab, getting out his phone. 'I'll set a timer.'

I arrange my cardy behind me and Fab spreads out his jacket, then we both lie back.

'Ready?'

I wriggle around until I'm comfy, then shut my eyes. 'Ready.'

'Go.'

For the first few seconds we don't say anything, and I just lie there, my face raised to the sun, listening to Fab's leather jacket squeaking and the birds singing.

'Fab,' I say, after a moment, 'I'm sorry about your mum and dad. It must suck having to choose between them.'

Our arms are just touching, and I suddenly want to hold his hand, but I don't because I'm worried it will send him the wrong message.

'It feels like something is missing all the time. I feel it

in Poland, and I feel it here …' He pauses, then adds, 'But I don't feel it right now.'

We settle into another silence. Somewhere near me a bee buzzes. The earth feels warm underneath me, like the very last bit of summer is in the soil.

This time it's Fab who breaks the silence. 'Annie, is it difficult having a disability?'

I'm so used to the direct way Fab asks questions that this doesn't even take me by surprise.

'I don't believe I have a disability,' I say.

'What do you mean?' Fab's voice floats across to me.

'I was born with cerebral palsy, which is a physical impairment, but my CP doesn't make me disabled: it's society that does that.'

Fab doesn't say anything, but even with my eyes closed I know that he's listening to me, trying to understand what I mean.

'Remember what happened on the bus?' I say. 'I could get out of my wheelchair, but if I hadn't been able to, and if the bus driver had refused to ask the women to fold up their pushchairs, then I would've had to get off the bus. It wouldn't have been my CP stopping me from getting that bus – it would have been society, because society thinks it's OK to prioritise the needs of able-bodied people on public transport. Some people think, at least there is space for wheelchairs – stop being so ungrateful. But how would non-disabled people feel if buses existed that only allowed wheelchair users inside with one or two seats reserved for non-disabled people? "Er, sorry, mate, I see you've got functioning legs. We just don't have the capacity for any more walkers on this bus. Look, we've already got one sitting in the corner."' I don't wait for Fab to answer. 'They'd feel excluded and angry.'

'You sound angry,' says Fab.

I am. 'Being disabled by the world does make me angry, but I'm less angry than I used to be … Or at least I've learnt to pick my battles.'

Fab doesn't say anything, but I can feel his arm warm against mine. The seconds tick by, then Fab says, 'You can be angry with me. Happy, angry, sad. I don't mind.'

I laugh. 'How about sleepy? Because these are the longest five minutes of my life. If I lie here another second I'm going to be snoring.'

'Ah,' says Fab. 'I might have stopped the timer.'

'What?!' I sit up and open my eyes. The world spins and everything – the fields, the trees, even Fab – is a washed-out, murky blue. I give him a thump on his arm. 'You idiot, Fab! Why did you do that?'

He laughs. 'I was enjoying talking … It doesn't matter. It still worked. Look how blue everything is.'

We're sitting so close to each other and I'm feeling so dizzy that it seems only natural to lean against Fab as I look around at the world that has become blue. He puts his arm round me.

'Let us record this beautiful moment of blueness,' he says, holding his phone in front of us.

I stay where I am as he presses the button to take our photo.

'Let's see.' I take the phone off him. 'Nice,' I say, passing it back.

Fab's arm stays round my shoulder. He's done this so many times before, but he's never felt this close, or lingered for so long. I rest against him for a moment longer, even though I know I should stop – because my leaning against him totally contradicts all the 'we're just friends' stuff I've been going on and on about – but I don't, because can't friends do this? Lean against each other in the sun?

I look up at him.

He smiles and I can't help smiling back.

'So …' I say.

'Yes?'

'You smell nice.' He does smell nice, sort of clean and bonfire-y.

'You smell nice too. Like *bez*. I do not know the word in English.'

Then it hits me. It would be so easy to kiss Fab right now. All I'd need to do is lean forward slightly and close my eyes. I know he'd kiss me back. I was sure I didn't like Fab, not like that, but he's really glowing in the afternoon light and his eyes match the colour of the sky almost perfectly …

What am I thinking?

I force myself to turn away and look at the view. But Fab is *still* staring at me and now there is absolutely no mistaking the kissing vibe that is building up. I tell myself that no matter how nice Fab smells, or how uncannily glowy he is, I must not kiss him. He would just expect so much to follow.

A few seconds tick by. The staring continues.

I have to do something *right* now to stop this. Lying down is not an option – that would seem like an invitation. Unfortunately standing up isn't an option either, because my legs have gone to sleep. So I do the only thing I can think of doing: I roll on to my front and start crawling up the hill to get away from him.

'*Bez* had better not be Polish for "cat sick",' I call over my shoulder. Then, just in case I haven't fully smashed up the romantic atmosphere, I add, 'Take me to the vegetarian sausages … I want a sausage!'

Oh, God. He's *still* watching me, all brooding and serious. Who does he think he is? Heathcliff?

So I hit him with my final passion-killer. 'Hurry up, Fab. I need a wee.'

Immediately, he jumps to his feet. 'Let's go.'

And the kissing vibe is not only dead – it's been trampled on and kicked into the nearest blackberry bush.

TWENTY-FIVE

At the barbecue, a deckchair's been reserved for me. I sit next to Fab's mum, work my way through my cheese and leek sausages and watch Fab.

Unlike most people our age, Fab doesn't change when he's around different people. He behaves in exactly the same way with Miss Caudle, Peggy, the Hoggers and, it appears, his family. Just like at college, he runs around organising and helping people, and occasionally doing something loud and embarrassing. At one point, he goes to fetch me some ketchup, a journey that takes a couple of minutes, and in this time he holds his niece upside down, turns the meat on the barbecue, stuffs some leaves down his uncle's top and sings a couple of lines of 'I Like to Move It' at the top of his voice, startling a couple who are walking their golden retriever.

Eventually, Fab settles next to me with a plate heaving

with kebabs and salad, and he gives me the low-down on his family.

'That girl with the pink coat is my niece, Paulina. She is seven and can do five cartwheels in a row. And that is Simon.' Fab points at a man frowning into the coals of the barbecue, tongs clasped in his hand. 'He is a British farmer going out with my cousin, Julia.' Next Fab nods at a boy sitting on a rug and sipping a bottle of Tyskie beer. 'Filip,' he says. 'He is on holiday from university, where he studies stones.'

'*Kości*,' says Fab's mum. She's been so quiet next to me that I'm startled when she speaks.

'Bones,' explains Fab. Then, after a quick conversation with his mum, he adds, 'Apparently I got it wrong. Filip is an archaeologist.'

After we've eaten more cake, everyone starts to pack up. Before I can climb back into Emil's van, Fab's mum presses a bag on me, saying, 'Blackberries and cake for your mother.'

Then she talks to Fab in Polish and this starts an animated discussion among everyone. The only people not joining in are me and English Simon.

'Annie,' she says, patting my arm, 'are you free on Saturday in two weeks?'

Unsure what I'm letting myself in for, I nod my head.

'Then you come with Fab to Simon and Julia's wedding!'

'Oh,' I say, trying to hide my alarm. 'Are you sure?'

'Yes,' she says, nodding and smiling.

Then everyone else joins in with the nodding and smiling.

I don't know what to say. Going to a wedding with Fab seems like such a massively girlfriendy thing to do, but I have to make up my mind because everyone is staring at me, waiting for an answer. Obviously I can't say, '*I'd like to come, but just to make it clear: I'm not going out with your son.*' So instead I say the first thing that pops into my head: 'I'm sorry, but I don't think I have the right clothes. The only shoes I have are trainers.'

For the first time this afternoon, English Simon decides to pipe up. 'I'm going to be wearing trainers,' he says.

Jeez. Thanks for nothing, Simon.

'Well, OK,' I say, fixing a big smile on my face. 'In that case, thank you. I'd love to come.'

General rejoicing breaks out and, despite my reservations, it's hard not to get swept up in the good mood.

Soon, Fab, Emil and I are in the van, and I'm waving goodbye to Fab's family.

As we drive out of the car park, Paulina runs after us shouting, 'See you at the wedding, Annie!'

'Don't worry,' says Fab, as we pull on to the road. 'Polish weddings are much better than English ones.'

'Why?' I ask.

'Vodka,' mutters Emil.

TWENTY-SIX

Once Mum went out with someone who was a
detective and he told me that a technique used
during questioning is to ask a suspect to explain what
happened chronologically, and then in reverse order.
Apparently it's harder to lie backwards.

This evening, it appears Mum is using this technique
on me.

'So what did you do again?' she asks, glancing up from
Poldark. She always watches reruns of *Poldark* on a
Sunday night and claims that looking at Captain Ross
is the only thing that takes her mind off work the
next day.

I stay focused on my phone. 'We picked blackberries,
ate cake, did the Blue Experience, had a barbecue, ate
cake, then I agreed to go to a wedding.'

She smiles and turns back to the screen. 'Remember

when you wore jeans to Auntie Jo's wedding and made her cry?'

'Yeah, well, her dress made me want to cry, but unlike her, I was too polite to do it.'

On the TV Ross and Demelza argue in a candlelit room.

'*Ahhh,*' sighs Mum. A few minutes later, she asks, 'What did you do after the blackberry-picking?'

'Ate.'

'And who was there?'

'Loads of Polish people. And English Simon.'

'Right …'

Ross and Demelza kiss … then argue … then kiss.

'And what's Fab's mum like?'

'Amazing. I love her. She hardly talks.'

Mum laughs. 'I'm only curious about what you got up to with this boy you've *never* mentioned before.'

'Well, suppress your curiosity.'

She looks back at the TV. Billowing white blouses are being tugged over heads and garments unlaced.

'Hello … here we go …' she mutters. Then, oh so casually, she adds, 'Anything like this happen when you were blackberry-picking?'

'*Mum*, Fab and I are just friends.' As I say the word *friends*, a pang of guilt creeps into me, because this wasn't entirely the message I gave Fab up on the hill. 'He definitely knows that's all we are,' I add. 'I've told him loads of times that I don't want to go out with him, or anyone for that matter!' By the end of my little speech, I'm not quite sure who it's aimed at: Mum, Fab … or me.

Mum's eyes are fixed on me. After a moment, she says, 'He seems like a really nice boy, Annie.'

'Yes. And your point is?'

'Be nice back to him, that's all.'

And that is my cue to jump to my feet. 'Goodnight, Mother.'

'Get away from the screen!' she yells as I walk past.

The next day, I'm sitting on the train with Jackson and we're doing our usual morning thing. He's messaging Amelia and I'm staring out of the window and fantasising about not getting off at college, just staying on the train and going somewhere I've never been before in my life. Maybe I'll carry on all the way to London, and from there I'll go by Eurostar to Paris. When I arrive, I'll just look up at the departure board and get the next train that's leaving. I could end up anywhere in Europe …

'Cows,' says Jackson, pointing out of the window, but without taking his eyes off his phone.

Sure enough, we're going past the field that's always

154

full of cows. Jackson and I have both got our favourites. Mine's number thirty-two, a skinny black cow who always scratches her bum on a broken fence, but never seems to be able to reach the right spot. One day, I'm going to go down there and give that cow a good old scratch myself.

'Well, well, well,' says Jackson, chuckling and glancing at me over the top of his phone. 'What have you been up to?'

I tear myself away from the itchy cow. 'What do you mean?'

'When were you going to mention that you're going out with Fab Kaczka?'

I burst out laughing. 'Never, because I'm *not* going out with Fab Kaczka.'

He raises one eyebrow. 'That's not what Snapchat's telling me.'

'Well, I wouldn't know about that because I'm not on Snapchat.'

'Oh yes you are,' he says, passing me his phone.

The picture Fab took of us on Saturday fills the screen. I'm resting against him and we're surrounded by the bright blue sky. *Moja Angielska dziewczyna!* is written in bouncy letters at the top of the screen.

I shrug. 'Don't be so infantile, Jackson. It's just a

picture. I've got hundreds of pictures of me and my rats on Facebook. Doesn't mean I'm dating them.'

He shrugs too and takes the phone back. 'True, but Fab has written "My English girlfriend" across your forehead, which kind of suggests that you're, you know, *his English girlfriend*.'

'What?' My stomach lurches. 'How do you know that's what it says?'

'Just Googled it.'

I force myself to laugh. 'Well, that's … bizarre. I wonder why he's saying that.'

'Who knows? He's an unpredictable guy.'

I sit back and look out of the window, really wishing Jackson would just disappear so I can get my head round this. A moment ago, I was looking forward to getting to college. I was looking forward to seeing Fab! Now I'm going to have to find him and sort this mess out.

'How come you know Fab anyway?' I ask Jackson.

'He's friends with everyone, plus we bonded over our mutual love of roast chicken.'

'Of course you did,' I say. 'Well, either Fab's joking or Google Translate isn't working properly because I am not Fab's girlfriend and he knows it.'

'Does he?' says Jackson. 'Because he's also changed his Facebook status to "In a relationship".' He looks up at me and laughs. 'Welcome to the couples club, Annie! Hang on ...' He starts tapping at his phone.

'What are you doing?'

'Asking him if he wants to go on a double date. You and Fab, me and Amelia, this Saturday, Nando's!'

I try to grab his phone, but he holds it just out of my reach and my attempts to get it make him laugh hysterically. After a few seconds of struggling, his phone pings and he reads the message.

'Fab says, "Yes, if Annie wants to go".'

I stare at him, open-mouthed. This perfectly sums up why I could never go out with Fab: my life would slip out of my control. It already is slipping out of my control! First, Fab announces to the world that I'm his girlfriend, and two minutes later I'm practically locked into a double date with Jackson and Amelia ... at Nando's!

'Well, tell Fab Annie *doesn't* want to go!'

Jackson laughs. 'Why not?'

I count the reasons off on my fingers. 'One, I'm a vegetarian and Nando's is quite meaty. Two, I'm going bowling with my mum on Saturday. And, three, I'm *not* going out with Fab!'

'Maybe you should give him a chance?'

I roll my eyes. 'Why? I already know I don't want to go out with him – I don't want to go out with anyone. Watching him eat flame-grilled chicken won't change that.'

'So ring him up and put him straight.'

'Oh, I'm going to put him straight,' I say, 'but I'm going to do it in person. Fab seems to find it difficult understanding my words, and it's got nothing to do with him being Polish.'

'Annie, do you want a chillax Chomp?' Jackson holds up a little chocolate bar.

Since I explained my mum's tendency to give me inspirational food, he's come up with a few of his own, for example, sadistic Skips and sexy Starburst. This is the first sensible suggestion he's had.

'I nicked it out of my brother's packed lunchbox, but I think you need it to help you get over the shock of almost being in a couple and not just thinking about yourself every second of the day.'

'Man, that's low,' I say, but I take the chocolate anyway because you should never turn down free chocolate.

I watch the cows and chomp on my Chomp. They look blissfully happy, independently munching grass in their field of freedom. I bet they never get some bull falsely claiming they belong to him and then advertising the fact on social media like they're some sort of trophy cow. Stupid, Annie, stupid. A bull wouldn't even be able to type with his cumbersome hooves. I stick the last bit of Chomp in my mouth just as the train pulls in to the station. The Chomp and my cow thoughts have cheered me up a bit.

Jackson and I get our stuff together.

'For the record, Annie,' he says, 'going out with someone isn't all about losing your freedom.'

'What is it about then?'

'*One*,' he ticks off a finger, mimicking me a moment ago, 'it's about always having someone comfy to lie on when you watch films. *Two*, it's about always being able to play two-player *Turtles in Time*. And finally, *three*, it's about having someone else's wardrobe to dip into.' The train comes to a halt and he jumps to his feet. 'Argue that, Demos!'

'One, I have cushions. Two, I don't even know what *Turtles in Time* is. And three, Jackson, *what are you talking about*? Don't tell me you're wearing something of Amelia's right now?'

He smiles. 'Oh yes I am!'

TWENTY-SEVEN

At college, I leave my wheelchair in my form room and go to find Fab.

He's leaning on the counter of the coffee shop, eating toast and flirting with Peggy. It's where he is most mornings, because Peggy lets him have the crusts half price. Today he's wearing his usual tracksuit bottoms and shirt combo. Plus espadrilles. I'm momentarily thrown from my kick-Fab's-butt resolve because his sleeves are rolled up and he does have exceptionally good arms. But as I walk across the room, I force myself to stare at his salmon-pink espadrilles. I need to stay focused.

'Annie!' he says. '*Piekna dziewczyna!*'

I roll my eyes. *Beautiful girl.* I suppose one upside to hanging out with this delusional person is that I'm learning Polish.

'You and me, Kazcka,' I say. 'We need to talk.'

He raises one eyebrow and puts down his buttery toast. 'Why? What has happened?'

'Er, you put a photo of us on Snapchat.' He looks confused, so I carry on, 'You know the one, Fab. You slapped "My English girlfriend" right across my face.'

'Aww, *sweet*!' says Peggy.

'Do you want some toast?' Fab holds out his paper plate. 'A hot chocolate?'

I shake my head. 'Stop trying to feed me up and just tell me what you were thinking.'

Fab glances at Peggy, who is standing watching us, her arms folded, obviously not going anywhere. 'Come with me,' he says.

I follow Fab to a sofa in the corner.

'Annie,' he says, the moment we're sitting down, 'what have I done wrong? You are angry about the picture? You don't like having pictures put online?'

'No, I don't, but the picture's not actually the problem, Fab. It's more the words.'

He leans back and throws his arms out wide. 'But I don't understand.'

'Fab, *I* am not your girlfriend and *you* are not my boyfriend, so don't tell people that we've got something special going on, because we haven't!' My mouth is on a roll now and it can't stop. 'I mean, when did that conversation happen? In between the cheese and leek sausages and *szarlotka*? Or was it during the Blue Experience? Was I so relaxed I fell asleep and you decided my snore meant *I want to go out with you?*'

He leans forward. 'But we were sitting so close and you said that I smelt nice.' He smiles. 'I added up the evidence!'

'You *added up the evidence*? Fab, I'm not *Wuthering Heights*. It was a nice afternoon, and I might have wanted another nice afternoon like it – as friends – but now I don't want to because you took some random events and concluded that we were dating. Then you announced it to the world! Fab, I don't like people telling me who I am!'

'Wait a minute, *random events*? Annie, we nearly kissed!' He looks right at me as he says this.

Over at the coffee shop, Peggy's mouth drops open.

'Does nothing embarrass you?' I hiss.

'Life is too short for embarrassment!'

'Yeah, you said.'

'Being with you, in the countryside, in the sun, cuddling. It was the best afternoon. I loved it!'

'We didn't *cuddle*, Fab. I rested against you. Cuddling involves arms and squeezing.'

'That,' he says, wagging his finger, 'is a mere technicality.'

'No,' I say, wagging my finger back, 'it's the truth. This is a rest …' I press my shoulder against his shoulder. 'And this is a cuddle …' I go to put my arms around him, but then I realise what I'm doing and let them fall back down by my side. 'Well, you get the idea.'

He leans back on the sofa again and frowns. 'No, I still don't understand. Show me what a cuddle is again.'

I can't help smiling. 'No way. You'll tell everyone we're engaged.'

With a shake of his head, Fab pulls out his phone. 'OK, OK, I will take the picture down.'

'And change your Facebook status.'

He raises his eyebrows. 'Fine.' A few seconds later, he puts his phone back in his pocket. 'It is all done. Now we will just wait and see what happens.'

He looks at me and I look at him, and I'm suddenly so aware of everything about him: his blue eyes, his hand that's resting on the seam of the sofa, his foot that's tapping up and down. My heart races and it's not just because I'm annoyed about the photo. It's also because, despite the espadrille that's jiggling up and down in front of my face, there's something I find a teeny bit attractive about Fab.

No! I need to put a stop to this flirting. Right now. Finding Fab a teeny bit attractive is not a good enough reason to give up my freedom. I find Jim a teeny bit attractive. I find the girl I sit next to in English language a teeny bit attractive. I even find Phil my sociology teacher a teeny bit attractive. It doesn't mean I should go out with any of them!

'Fab, *nothing* is going to happen. I like you and we had a really good afternoon together, but that doesn't mean I'm ever going to be your girlfriend.'

'Annie, I promise I will never call you my girlfriend again.'

'But you still want a girlfriend, don't you? *Your girl?* Someone who you can look after and take on dates and show off to the world?'

'What's wrong with that?' asks Fab. 'If you were my girlfriend I would want to take you to wonderful places. I would be proud to go out with you. I'd *want* to show you off to the world!'

Automatically, an image springs into my mind of Fab parading me around the common room. 'I'd hate that,' I burst out. 'I don't want to be shown off like a new pair of shoes!'

'I care nothing about shoes,' he says, entirely missing the point.

'Look, Fab, starting college is a big deal for me. It's the most freedom I've ever had in my life, and I want to enjoy it without the complication of being someone's girlfriend. Why's that so hard to understand?'

Fab doesn't look convinced. 'I suppose because I do not believe it would be a complication. But I think I do understand. I think maybe you want someone who isn't me. *I'm* the complication.' His smile is fading and, although he doesn't move his arm, that feeling that's buzzing between us … it fades a little bit too.

I shake my head. 'No, I don't want to be involved with anyone right now. At all.'

'So you will not come to the wedding with me?'

'No. It's not a good idea, but please say thank you to Julia and Simon for asking me.'

He puts his hands on his knees and stares at them. Then he nods. 'I'm sorry I embarrassed you with the picture and the words. From now on, we are Annie and Fab, friends.' He holds out his hand. 'Put it here, my friend.'

I put my hand in his and he squeezes it. We're supposed to be saying hello, but for some reason this feels like we're saying goodbye.

'So everything is OK,' I say, trying to read his face. 'You and me? We're OK?'

'Of course.' He jumps to his feet. 'We can pretend that yesterday never happened.' He pauses here to give me one last look. 'Now, before I go to my maths lesson I must collect up the empty cups for Peggy.'

'I'll help.'

He shakes his head. 'It's OK. I can do it on my own.'

I look round the room. He's right: he doesn't need me. 'See you in English?'

He does a quick salute. 'See you in English, Annie, my friend and nothing more.' Then he's off, scooping up mugs and stacking them under his chin.

TWENTY-EIGHT

Over the next few days, Fab diligently behaves like my friend and absolutely nothing more.

He still sits next to me in English and we talk, and argue, but I don't get any more *moja dziewczyna*s, and it might be my imagination, but Fab doesn't really seem to come over and chat to me in the common room, and he chats to *everyone* in the common room. I mean, on Wednesday, I even saw him playing chess with briefcase boy from my form.

I tell myself this is good, and I focus on hanging out with my friends, enjoying my freedom and doing what I want when I want. Although now I'm being such a good friend to Hilary, I also have to do quite a bit of what she wants too. And what she wants to do on Thursday is feed the ducks in the park near college. The boys come along too, because the cafe in the park sells such good paninis.

'I told you you'd love it,' Hilary says, attempting to stroke a scruffy-looking mallard. 'Look at their cute faces!

'They've got mites,' Oliver says. 'I can tell by the way they're nibbling their feathers.'

Jim backs away from an aggressive seagull who wants in on the action. 'You are such a buzzkill, Oli. You know that, right?'

'I'm a realist, which is why I'm not having a party when my parents go away.'

I look up from the group of ducks surrounding my wheelchair. 'Who's having a party when their parents go away?'

Jim says, 'Oli. His mum and dad are going off to watch *Les Misérables* and stay in a Travelodge. They're practically begging us to have a party.'

'It would almost be rude not to,' I say.

Hilary grabs Oliver's hand. 'Please, Oli,' she says, pushing her glasses up her nose so that they really maximise the size of her eyes. 'I really like parties.'

I don't believe it. Hilary's actually working Oliver!

After a moment's hesitation, he pulls his hand away. 'No. The last time I had a party the police were called and it was all Mal's fault.'

We turn to look at Mal, who has his mouth full of panini.

He nods to let us know this is true.

'What happened?' I ask.

'So I had a superhero party –'

'For his *sixteenth* birthday,' says Jim, grinning.

'I was, and still am, very into comics,' says Oliver, without a trace of embarrassment, 'and I wanted an excuse to wear my Batman costume. It's made of leather.'

'Oh, wow.' I gaze at Oliver with new-found respect. 'Tell me you wear that costume when you're killing vermin?'

'Of course not,' he says, frowning. 'It's very expensive. Mal came to my party dressed as Jack Sparrow, ignoring the very clear *superhero* costume instructions on the invitation.'

'And he decides to try alcohol for the first time,' says Jim, taking over. 'He raids Oli's parents' drinks cabinet then wanders outside. Next thing we know, a neighbour's knocking on the door in his pyjamas and he's got Captain Jack in an armlock. Then the police turn up!'

'Apparently I went into the neighbour's house,' says Mal.

'They came downstairs to find a pirate drinking a pint of their milk and dancing around the kitchen to Sting,' says Jim. He's laughing so much he's alarming the ducks.

'Apparently I put the radio on,' adds Mal.

'Oliver, you have *got* to have a party,' I say. 'If your last one was that good, imagine what this one will be like!'

Mal says, 'We could do superheroes again. You'd get to be Batman, Oli …'

Oliver bites his lip and we can see that he's tempted.

'I'll help tidy up,' adds Hilary. 'I won't go home until your house is spotless.'

Slowly, Oliver nods. 'OK, next Friday, superhero party at my place, but you've got to promise to keep it small.'

We all yell, sending the ducks flying into the air.

'Avian flu!' shouts Jim. 'Cover your mouths!' Then he crouches close to me. 'I am so putting it on Facebook.'

'It's going to be massive,' I say, and we share a look of wicked complicity.

TWENTY-NINE

We spend Friday lunchtime in the common room discussing the important issue of costumes. Oliver's just explaining exactly who Bushmaster is (a human being with cybernetic arms and tails, *obviously*), when Uncle Emil walks into the canteen with his toolbox. He's followed by Fab, who's staggering under the weight of a huge cardboard box. This should be a surprising sight, but I became immune to the surprising things Fab does a long time ago.

'What's your boyfriend up to now?' says Jim.

Before I can answer, or even hit him on the arm, Hilary says, 'Fab's got permission to set his table football up in here. He told me about it in French.'

I feel a flicker of irritation that Fab didn't tell *me* about his table football, but I remind myself not to be stupid. Why should he have mentioned it to me? Didn't I make it very clear that I'm not his girl?

171

Fab starts pulling handles out of the box covered in little football players, and Hilary announces, 'I'm going to be Squirrel Girl.'

'You've made that up,' says Jim.

'Ah, she hasn't, actually,' says Oliver. 'Squirrel Girl first appeared in 1992 in a Marvel comic drawn by Steve Ditko.'

'Her costume's all furry.' Hilary gives herself a cuddle in anticipation.

'What's Squirrel Girl's power?' I ask.

'She can communicate with squirrels,' says Hilary.

'Rubbish superpower,' muses Mal.

'Says the man who's never encountered an angry squirrel,' says Oliver, darkly. 'They bite to the bone.'

Over in the centre of the room, Emil starts shouting at Fab and waving a screwdriver in his face. Today Fab is dressed from head to toe in black Adidas. His tracksuit top is zipped up high and he's rolled up his sleeves. Pushed to the back of his head is a black beanie. If he wasn't wearing his espadrilles, he'd look like a ninja.

'Annie!' Jim's clicking his fingers in front of his face. 'Which superhero are you going to be?'

'Hit-Girl,' I say. 'I've always wanted an excuse to wear a purple wig.'

We chat about wigs and tights for a bit longer, then

Jim gets to his feet. 'I'll see you dudes later. I've got a driving lesson.'

'Seriously?' Mal looks amazed. 'Why didn't you tell us?'

'Because you'd want to watch me drive out of college and that would put me off.'

Mal grabs Oliver. 'Let's watch him drive out of college and put him off.'

Jim groans and runs out of the common room with Mal and Oliver close behind him.

'I like them,' I say. 'Don't you?'

'Yeah,' says Hilary, wrinkling her nose. 'They're cute.'

We sit back on the sofa and soak up the great Friday feeling that's sweeping the common room. Everyone's in a good mood and the iPod Hoggers have even allowed some popular music to be played.

Soon the football table has been constructed and Fab tests each handle in turn, making the players spin round.

Next to me, Hilary sighs. 'I am so disappointed about you two.'

'What?' I glance across at her.

'You and Fab. I was shipping you guys so hard.'

'Well, you picked the wrong couple to ship.'

I break a corner off my waffle and watch as Fab says goodbye to his uncle, shaking his hand and then giving

173

him a bear hug. It looks like the table's ready for its first match.

'Scarlett,' Fab calls out, 'come and play!'

I watch as the Hogger with the achingly cool short hair jumps up and goes to stand next to Fab. Two of Scarlet's friends take the opposite side of the table.

Fab drops the ball into the centre, and they're off, spinning the handles, yelling and swearing (with the exception of Fab). Scarlett clearly isn't in full control of her goalie because Fab keeps having to reach round her to get to it.

Suddenly, Hilary says, 'So if you don't like him, how come you're stalking him with your eyes?'

'What?' I turn to see her looking at me and smiling. 'I am not! He's hard to avoid, that's all. He's tall … and so loud. If a double-decker bus honked its horn, you'd look at it, right?'

They must have scored because Fab's roaring in delight and hugging Scarlett.

'Well, if your eyes were a tongue,' says Hilary, 'then you'd have licked Fab to death in the past five minutes.'

'Ew, Hilary. First of all, gross. Secondly, *shut up*! What are you on about?'

'Are you eating that?' She nods towards the waffle on my plate.

'No. All your licking talk has made me lose my appetite.'

She picks it up and takes a bite. 'It's just, I've been watching you, and thinking that maybe you kind of like Fab and you're feeling a bit jealous.'

I burst out laughing. 'Sorry to disappoint you, but, no, I haven't suddenly developed a thing for sportswear combined with excessive height.'

She shrugs. 'Must have misread the signals,' she pops the last bit of my waffle into her mouth, 'because that's *exactly* what I thought you were into.' She jumps to her feet. 'Gotta go. I've got a book waiting for me at the library. You coming?'

I think about all the stairs that would involve and how jelly-like my legs feel right now and the fact that my wheelchair is currently on the opposite side of college. 'No, thanks. Sofa's too comfy.'

Then I'm all alone. Just me and my thoughts and a noisy game of table football. And my thoughts get massively stuck on what Hilary just said. I stare at Scarlett. Right now, her pretty little head is flung back and she's laughing at the top of her voice. She deliberately bumps against Fab with her hip, pushing him away from the table with her tiny denim-encased bottom. She's also wearing chunky boots and an enormous cardigan. She looks amazing … Cow.

Oh, God. I have just called a girl I have never spoken to *a cow*. Hilary's right ... I must be jealous!

The thought makes me sit up a little taller because if I'm jealous of Scarlett then Hilary's right about that other thing too: I must like Fab. That's how jealousy works! Immediately, I feel slightly sick and start to blush, even though I'm sitting all on my own and no one is watching me. Clearly, I've got a problem with the idea, but I force myself to run with it, just for a moment, so I can work out exactly what my mind is playing at.

Say I do like Fab. I know he likes me so it would be simple, wouldn't it? I'd just go up to him and say, 'Hey, Fab, I've got the hots for you. Let's go out.' I could do it today. 'Sure thing,' he'd say – conveniently forgetting everything I said to him on Monday – then he'd wrap his big arms around me, pulling me close, and I'd slip my arms round him and our whole bodies would touch, and ...

No. *No way*. It would get so intense so quickly. Fab isn't the sort of person who does things by halves. He'd expect to hold hands, sit next to me in the common room, text me, ring me, know what I'm thinking and feeling every moment of the day. I'd become Fab's girl. I'd become *Fannie*.

I push the liking Fab thing into a corner of my mind and I lock it away ... then I throw away the key.

Straight away, I feel better, lighter.

'Annie!' I look up and see Fab standing in front of me with a big smile on his face. 'Coming to English?'

'Yes, I am!' I say, a bit too brightly.

'Are you OK?' he asks. 'You look red.'

'Do I?' I look down as I gather up my stuff. 'Well, it's hot in here, don't you think?'

'No.'

Urrgh! Why does he have to always speak the truth?

'Well, I'm wearing layers. Layers make me hot, but cosy, you know?' Wow. I need to stop talking. 'And that's why I'm red. Layers. So. English. Shall we go?'

He smiles and shrugs. 'I'm waiting for you.'

'Oh yes!' I say, then I laugh a little too brightly and for a little too long.

THIRTY

I spend the weekend making my Hit-Girl costume and trying and failing not to think about Fab. It doesn't help that we've got an essay due in and he sends me a series of *Wuthering Heights*–related texts. They're all very businesslike – Annie, exactly how old is Heathcliff when he leaves Wuthering Heights?; Annie, when does Catherine marry Edgar? – but they have the effect of turning my bedroom into the common room. Fab just keeps popping up all the time, and each time my phone pings I get this little flutter of anticipation and I blush.

I blush on my own *in my bedroom*!

But I tell myself Hilary's wrong. I'm not acting like this because I'm lusting after Fab – I'm simply addicted to the constant attention he'd been giving me. I don't like the taste of Pringles and I know they're not good for me, but once I've put one in my mouth I can't stop eating them. I'm addicted to Fab, that's all, and I need to get him out of my system. I need a Fab detox.

I decide that the party is the perfect Fabstraction – after all, he's already told me he can't go – so when I'm back at college I throw myself into planning Oliver's party.

I say 'Oliver's party', but really it's become *our* party. We decide on a guest list (modest), food (pizza and crisps), drink (whatever everyone brings) and we finalise the dress code (if you're not in a leotard and/or tights then you're not coming in). Soon we've got Oliver to agree to a giant spider's web in his kitchen, 'kryptonite' jelly and a load of props for a selfie booth.

On Thursday, I'm so busy sewing sequins on Jim's duvet cover (it's going to be his Robin cape) that I don't even notice Fab presenting Peggy with a birthday cake until everyone starts singing 'Happy Birthday'. Progress!

The party planning goes well until Oliver gets cold feet on Friday lunchtime.

'Mum collects owls and Dad grows bonsai,' he says, nibbling fiercely on a carrot. 'If loads of people come tonight then something will get broken.'

'Oli, calm down,' says Jim. 'Loads of people are not going to be a problem. We're just not that popular. More likely it's just going to be us five sitting around your living room, wearing masks and admiring your dad's tiny trees.'

'And fighting our way out of the spider's web,' adds Hilary.

Oli gasps. 'You see? These things get out of hand!'

'Only if someone puts an invitation on Facebook,' says Jim. 'Which we haven't done, have we, Mal?'

Mal shakes his head solemnly. 'And we didn't stand up and tell everyone in our maths group about it either.'

Oliver's eyes widen in alarm, so I add, 'And we've *definitely* not stuck up posters on the doors of the girls' toilets.'

'Or told my brother, who hangs out with some really badass drug dealers who fight with Clocks,' says Hilary.

'Don't you mean *Glocks*?' says Jim, smiling.

Hilary nods. 'Yeah, that's what I said, *Clocks*!'

'Don't joke about badass drug dealers,' says Oliver. 'One of Mum's owls is Murano glass. It's very rare and expensive. A drug dealer would probably love to get their hands on it.'

'Unfortunately we are joking,' says Jim, sighing and running his hands through his already messed-up hair. 'I'm not sure we can even call it a party. Do ten people in a room make a party, or is it a gathering?' He nods towards me and Hilary. 'I think you two are the only girls going.'

'We're all you need,' I say, smiling.

'Annie,' says Mal, 'have you asked Fab?' He nods across the common room to where Fab is playing a solo game of table football, leaning across the table to operate both teams. I'm afraid I noticed this some time ago, but in my defence he is talking to himself, loudly.

'Fab's busy,' I say.

He's going to Simon's stag do, which is obviously excellent news because I can't detox from Fab if he's handing out pizza dressed as Wolverine. I'm not sure why I've just imagined Fab dressed as Wolverine, but suddenly it's a powerful image and I'm looking at Fab and picturing it in vivid detail: the vest, the jeans, the shiny belt buckle ... What's wrong with me? I'm supposed to be weaning myself off Fab, not imagining him in a skin-tight vest!

'This party is going to be great,' I say, tearing my eyes away. Then I add, in a loud and confident voice, 'And we definitely don't need Fab to be there.'

'If there's one person I actually want at my party, it's Fab,' Oliver mutters.

'Why?' I burst out. 'He's not that great!'

He looks at me. 'Yes. He is. People listen to Fab. If Fab says, "Don't touch the tiny trees" then *no one* will touch the tiny trees.'

'Oliver, people listen to me too, and I can protect those bonsai.'

He nods. 'I suppose so … But Fab's got this presence –'

I roll my eyes. 'He's got a big voice, that's all.'

On cue, Fab yells out, '*GOL!*'

'Oliver, no one's touching those little trees,' I say, 'not on my watch. And we don't need Fab Kaczka's magical presence in our lives!'

The four of them look at me, frowning.

'At the party. We don't need his magical presence at the party. Tonight.'

The boys nod, but Hilary keeps looking at me, eyes narrowed, with a smile playing on her lips.

THIRTY-ONE

Seven hours later, I'm in Oliver's back garden, and Hilary and I are trying to prune the little trees with a teeny-weeny pair of scissors.

'Look at me: I'm a giant!' I say, snipping at a leaf.

'Annie!' Oliver appears next to us. 'Put the scissors down!'

At least, I *think* it's Oliver. We arrived early to help get things ready and Oliver was so busy putting peanuts in bowls and hiding owls that he wasn't in costume. Well, he is definitely In Costume now, and we're talking head-to-foot, encased-in-black-leather In Costume. And he didn't just tell me off in his normal voice – he used *Batman's* voice!

This is the best party I've ever been to in my life, and Fab's nowhere near it. I'm cured!

Oliver's parents live on a sort of farm so we're in the middle of nowhere, running round a slightly spooky old

183

house, dressed up as superheroes. Plus there are animals all over the place. I've already stroked a dog, two cats, a mink and a chicken. Jim immediately took over the living room and 'made it mellow' with candles and some 'gnarly techno rhythms'. In fact, it's so gnarly that Hilary and I decided to give our ears a rest in the garden, which is how we discovered the bonsai collection.

'Squirrel Girl told me to do it,' I say, pointing at Hilary.

'Well, the squirrels told *me* to do it!' Hilary is wearing a brown onesie with six 'squirrels' sewn on it. All of the squirrels are teddy bears with added tails. And then there's *the* tail. Hilary is not going to be doing much sitting tonight.

'Well, you're banned from the garden,' growls Batman/Oliver. 'Get in the Bat Cave!'

As we weave our way back up the garden, Hilary leans against me and whispers, 'Is it just me, or has Oliver increased his sexiness by about one thousand per cent just by dressing up as Batman?'

'I can hear everything you're saying,' says Oliver, still with the growl, 'because I'm standing next to you. Plus a thousand per cent doesn't exist.'

'Oh yeah!' says Hilary, then she doubles over and giggles so hard all her squirrels shake.

It's fair to say that Hilary is in a very silly mood. I'm also in a silly mood, fuelled almost entirely by my mad desire to forget about Fab.

'Don't do anything silly,' said Mum when she dropped us off. My God, the woman's a mind reader.

We follow Oliver into the front room and he stands in there, arms folded, legs astride, looking around with satisfaction. There are about twenty people crammed into the room: our group, a few boys from Oliver's old school and some people from college. There's talking, laughing, a bit of dancing (Mal) and in a corner a noisy game of Dobble is taking place. It really is a very civilised party/gathering.

I grab another Fanta from a tub of icy water by the fireplace. I need something to wake me up and these Fantas have got my name written all over them – literally, with a red Sharpie.

I drop down on the sofa just as Jim comes in, carrying two green jellies.

'Ah, Robin,' says Oliver, arms still folded. 'I see you have brought the kryptonite jelly.'

'Don't speak to me like I'm your sidekick,' says Jim, dumping one jelly on the table then sitting next to me.

Jim's Robin costume consists of a lady's green swimming costume worn over tights with his sequinned duvet cover draped over his shoulders. Every time I look at him I laugh.

'Don't laugh,' he says, passing me a Dorito. 'Eat jelly instead. This is your spoon.'

The lime jelly goes surprisingly well with the Dorito and soon I've polished off a handful of Doritos and half the jelly. Suddenly, I notice that Jim's watching me.

'What?' I say.

'That wig. It makes you look different.'

'Yeah? Different how?'

'I dunno. Like I'm talking to Annie's hot big sister.'

'OK, that was a double-edged compliment, but never mind because I *love* your jelly. It's so moreish!'

'That'll be the vodka,' he says.

I pause, my jelly-loaded Dorito halfway to my mouth. 'Really?'

'Why would I bring just jelly?'

'Er, because it tastes nice?' I consider putting the jelly back, but then it would be covered in my crisp crumbs, plus I am enjoying it. 'I guess a bit won't make me lose my balance entirely.'

'Nah,' says Jim. 'You'll be fine.'

'But what about the gelatine? I'm a vegetarian and I've just eaten, like, a fistful of cow jelly.'

'But it tastes so good!' says Jim, balancing more jelly on a Dorito and moving it slowly towards my mouth.

And that's all the encouragement I need to throw my principles to one side, open my mouth and get stuck into a load of vodka, sugar and cow jelly.

THIRTY-TWO

At some point, the overhead light gets turned off, a lava lamp is turned on and the music is changed. I dance with Hilary and Mal. Jim puts on Oliver's mum's sheepskin coat, then I sit on the sofa and just watch the party taking place around me. The hot girl from my English language class starts to dance in circles in the middle of the rug. She's wearing a Catwoman mask and a cape which spins round and round with her. She's making me feel dizzy so I shut my eyes.

When I open them again, Jim's sitting next to me making shapes with his hands in the air. He sees me watching him and freezes.

'Why did you stop?' I ask.

'Because you made me embarrassed.'

'Jim, life's too short for embarrassment,' I say, and I realise I've repeated word for word what Fab said to me. I even wagged my finger. How annoying: I just relapsed.

'Isn't embarrassment just your body's early-warning system that you're making a fool of yourself?' asks Jim.

I shake my head. 'No, it's your body's early-warning system that you care too much about what people think.'

Jim puts his feet up on the coffee table. 'But I don't care what people think.'

I laugh. 'Jim, you hate looking stupid. That's why you make sure you like bands and clothes and comedians that are all just the right side of eccentric.'

'Annie.' He turns to look at me. 'I'm wearing my sister's swimming costume and my mum's tights. I'm at peace with looking stupid.'

'But we're all supposed to be wearing stuff like that tonight. Don't worry about it, Jim.' I give his knee a pat. 'You're a conformist. It's not a crime. But look at Oliver ...' Right now, Oliver is dancing in role as Batman and he's doing these weird swoopy movements across the room, crouching up and down and jumping on and off a sofa. 'He's the real deal. He never fakes it ... Unlike you.'

'Now you're just trying to wind me up.'

I am, just a bit.

'How can I prove it to you that I'm not a conformist faker?'

'Ah,' I say, 'that's tricky, because if I suggest something – like put on Rihanna and robot dance – and you do it, well, you'd just be *conforming* to what I expected, wouldn't you? Like a big fat faker.'

'So I'm trapped.'

'I'm afraid so, but don't worry.' I pat his cheek. 'I still love you.'

'Unless …' he narrows his eyes, 'I do something that genuinely surprises you.'

At some point during the last five minutes, Jim and I have sort of squished together on the sofa. It's a squishy sofa, but I could have resisted the squish if I'd really wanted to. I register all this somewhere at the back of my mind as Jim and I look at each other, our faces very close together.

'My mum's coming to pick me and Hilary up in an hour,' I say, 'so you have sixty minutes to surprise me.'

'I only need one minute,' he says, not taking his eyes off me.

Now our faces are so close together that I can see the golden flecks in his brown eyes. Someone's put on one of Oliver's parents' Beatles CDs, 'Here Comes the Sun'.

'Go on then,' I say. 'Surprise me.'

And just like I know he's going to, he leans forward, puts one hand on the side of my face and kisses me.

189

Finally, I think, as I kiss him back, proof that I don't like Fab.

I hear someone – Oliver? – laughing, but we don't stop kissing because very quickly the joke kiss turns into a real kiss, and I'm grabbing hold of the sheepskin coat Jim's wearing and pulling him to me. And it's lovely being wrapped tight against someone with my eyes closed. Then, in a distant part of my brain, I realise that although my lips are touching Jim's lips and my hands are buried in Jim's hair, I'm not thinking about Jim at all.

I'm thinking about Fab.

Fab's lips, Fab's arms, Fab's Bombay Sapphire eyes. I'm imagining that I'm kissing Fab!

I pull away from Jim so quickly that I leave my wig in his hand.

'What's the matter?' he asks.

I stare at him and all I can think is: I like Fab. How could I have been so stupid? *I like Fab!*

'Hello?' He puts my wig back on my head. 'Earth to Annie!'

'Speaking!' I say, forcing myself to smile. 'Sorry, I got distracted.'

'By my amazing surprise?'

'Yep,' I say, nodding.

190

I guess I must look a bit intense because Jim says, 'That didn't mean anything, right?'

I shake my head. 'No way. I only kissed you because of the swimming costume.'

He laughs, clearly relieved. 'Good. I mean, you look hot and everything, but I think that's mainly down to the wig, and you can't wear that all the time. Good kiss though?'

I nod. 'Good kiss. Very … surprising … Now I need some crisps.'

I get to my feet, wobble, and Jim pushes my bum to stop me from falling back down.

A few moments later, I find myself dancing round the room with Hilary to 'I Saw Her Standing There'.

'What was that all about?' she asks.

'Oh … nothing.'

She bursts out laughing. 'Really? It didn't look like nothing.'

And I suppose that's true, because that kiss was nothing and everything all at the same time, but I don't get the chance to even think about this because suddenly someone shouts, 'Mal's put a chicken in the spider's web!' and there's a stampede into the kitchen.

THIRTY-THREE

When I wake up the next morning, a storm is blowing outside, and my mind is in similar chaos.

Luckily, Hilary's lying like a starfish on the airbed next to me so I have instant access to counselling.

'Hilary,' I whisper, 'are you awake?'

No. Clearly she isn't. Her mouth is hanging open and she's drooling. I lean over and give her a gentle shake.

'Hilary, please wake up. It's an emergency.'

'What?!' She jerks awake and looks around, confused.

'Hilary, I need to talk to you.'

She picks up her phone. 'At *seven twenty-three*?'

'Yes,' I say.

'Just let my eyes open,' she says, blinking, then rubbing them, then blinking again. She pulls her glasses on. 'OK, they're open. What's so urgent?'

I curl up on my side so that we're facing each other. 'I'm feeling pretty bad about last night.'

'The Jim kiss?'

I nod, and Hilary reaches over and pats my shoulder.

'Don't worry about it, Annie.'

'You're right – I shouldn't worry about it. I mean, if I can't have stupid kisses now, then when can I have them? And it was such a little kiss –'

Hilary laughs. 'It wasn't *that* little. It began during "Here Comes the Sun", then I sat on a doughnut, went to the toilet, peeled off the doughnut and washed the jam off, and when I came back the kiss was *still* going on!'

I groan. 'Not making me feel better, Hilary.'

'Oh yeah … Sorry.'

'Urrgh.' I pull a pillow over my head. 'I feel sick. I mean, it might be the jelly, but I'm fairly certain it's because of the kiss.'

'But why is it making you feel sick? Jim's really nice.'

I peek out from the pillow. 'I'm thinking maybe I feel so bad because of … Fab?'

She frowns. 'But why would you feel bad about Fab? How many times have you told me that you don't like him … unless …' She sits bolt upright. 'You *do* like him? I knew it! My love radar is not defective!'

'*Love?* Hilary, don't say things like that! Call it a *like* radar. I like him. I accept it. When I was kissing Jim all I could think about was Fab. You're so right – I do look at Fab all the time. I've tried not to, but I can't stop myself. He's like Pringles.' Hilary frowns, but I just carry on. 'The Jim kiss was supposed to prove I didn't like Fab, but it didn't work. It just made me want Fab more than anything!'

'But I thought you didn't want a boyfriend.'

'I don't. That's why I'm groaning. I want Fab, but not all the heavy stuff that would involve.'

'How do you know it would involve heavy stuff? Have you ever asked him?'

I think for a moment. 'No, but I can just tell. He's so old-fashioned. The other week in English he told me he's looking forward to getting married!'

'So am I,' she says. 'In about twenty years! Look, maybe you don't have to be Fab's girlfriend. You could be his something else. Just tell him you like him and then talk about it.'

I emerge from my pillow. 'You really think I should do that?'

'Yes! You like him and he likes you. One thing I know about Fab is that he's a kind person. Just tell him everything you've told me – well, except for the bit about Jim, obviously.'

Suddenly, everything seems clearer. She's right. I do just need to talk to Fab. I've been making assumptions about him, something that drives me mad when people do it to me. But I can't wait until Monday. Fab's like human sunshine: I need the reassuring glow I get from him right now. I sit up and smile.

'Today's Saturday, the day of the wedding. Shall I go to the wedding and tell him there?'

'Oh my God, yes!' She nearly claps her hands with excitement. 'Ring him!'

'I can't. I left my phone at Oliver's.'

She hands me her phone. 'Use mine. His number's under BFG.'

I find the BFG's number and take one last look at Hilary. 'You really think this is the right thing to do?'

This time Hilary really does clap her hands. 'Definitely!'

I take a deep breath as the phone rings once, then twice.

'Hilary!' Fab sounds wide awake.

'Actually, it's Annie. I mean, I'm using Hilary's phone.' I say all this in a rush.

'Annie?'

Is it my imagination or has his voice gone a bit flat? I decide it's my imagination and push on. 'It's about the wedding. I'd really like to come, if I'm still invited.' Down on the floor, Hilary gives me a thumbs up, but the sound of wind and rain falling on the window fills the silence on the other end of the phone. 'But if it's a problem, Fab, don't worry about it.'

'No, of course it is not a problem. My family would love you to come.'

'Really?'

He laughs. 'Really! Sorry, I was not expecting you to change your mind.'

'Well … I haven't seen you much since we went blackberry-picking.' I take a breath, then add, 'I guess I've missed you.'

Opposite me Hilary clutches her hands together and mouths, 'Love it!'

Again, Fab goes quiet, before saying, 'I've missed you too.' He sounds sad, totally unlike Fab, and for a moment I wonder if I've left it too late. If Fab's already given up on me. 'I'll text the details to Hilary. I'm pleased you are coming, Annie.'

'So?' says Hilary the moment I hang up.

'It's fine. All sorted,' I say, nodding to convince myself this is true.

'What now?' She puts her arms above her head and does a big stretch. 'Seeing as you've woken me up ridiculously early, we might as well do something.'

I push my worries to the back of my mind. 'We're going to take our duvets downstairs and I'm going to make us some toast and then we're going to eat the toast watching endless episodes of *Friends*. Then we're going shopping to buy me some shoes.'

Hilary flops back on the airbed. 'Best weekend ever!'

THIRTY-FOUR

The wedding reception is being held in a barn deep in the countryside and when we eventually find it, Mum pulls up as close to the entrance as possible. She was surprised when I told her I'd changed my mind about the wedding, but when I said it was important and gave her a meaningful look, she agreed to miss *Strictly Come Dancing* to drive me here.

'You OK to get a taxi back?' she asks.

I nod, and look at the silver and purple balloons tied around the door to the barn. The storm has faded away, but the balloons are blowing wildly in the wind and there are still dark clouds in the sky. I put my hand on the door handle, but I don't open it.

'Feeling shy?' Mum says.

More scared, I think, as I stare at the crowd of people milling around the barn door.

'Look, I don't know why you changed your mind about going to this wedding, but whatever or whoever the reason is, it was enough to make you get all dressed up and wear shoes so it must be important.'

'It is important,' I say, turning to look at her. '*He's* important.

Mum's been waiting so long for a moment like this that I really admire her restraint. She doesn't gasp, or try to hug me – in fact, she doesn't do anything except sit there and wait for me to carry on talking.

I look back out of the window. 'Fab likes me. He's told me that he thinks we'd be perfect together. One week, he even asked me out every single day, like on a proper date, and that's how we ended up going blackberry-picking. Other people think we'd be perfect together too. They've even given us a name: Fannie.'

'Sounds kind of intense, but also kind of lovely.'

'Exactly.' I keep my eyes fixed on the windscreen, watching as people move in and out of the barn. 'I do like him, but I'm scared about what might come next.'

Mum laughs. 'Fab might want to watch the *Final Destination* films with you.'

'I hate the *Final Destination* films.'

'I know, and he might want to hold your hand all the time.'

'My skin prickles when even *you* hold my hand.'

She nods. 'And he might call you "sweetheart".'

I shudder. A consultant once called me 'sweetheart' so I called him 'darling' back. Mum definitely found it funnier than he did.

'You would lose control, just a bit,' says Mum. 'That's what happens when you're in a relationship. You might love it. You might hate it. But you'll never know if you run away from what you're feeling.'

'I feel like I'm changing already, Mum. I don't know who I am. I'm like the Incredible Hulk, but I'm not turning green and massive – I'm turning … *romantic*!'

She laughs and takes my hand. 'Annie, you know who you are. You'll never lose yourself.'

Slowly, I feel my fear lifting and being replaced by something else. Excitement? Energy? I do feel like the Incredible Hulk, but in a good way!

'Need a Courage Kiss?' Mum says.

I'm about to remind her that I haven't willingly accepted Courage Kisses for over five years, but then I realise a Courage Kiss is just what I need so I offer her my cheek. 'Put it here. Make it a big one.'

Mum gives me a kiss. 'Fight the fear, beautiful girl!'

I nod, then get out of the car. Mum hands me my

crutches from the back seat. I don't want them, but I know I need to use them.

I watch Mum drive away, then crunch my way across the gravel, really wishing that for once I could make a quiet entrance. Mind you, if I'd wanted to make a quiet entrance, I wouldn't have worn velvet shoes and a silver dress. At least I match the balloons.

Inside, the barn looks magical: fairy lights are twisted through trailing ivy and a band is playing on a stage.

I see Fab straight away, dancing with some little girls. I watch him for a moment. He's obviously been wearing a suit, but he's lost the jacket and now his tie is wonky and his sleeves are rolled up. Those arms. They make me feel a bit weak inside … I mean, even weaker than I already feel.

When Fab sees me, he waves and walks over.

'Hello,' he says, stopping in front of me.

'Hi,' I say.

We stand there facing each other, and I suddenly feel overwhelmed by uncertainty. I feel like I need to give him some explanation about why I changed my mind, but at the same time I can't bring myself to say all that, not now. I need to find the right moment.

Luckily, Fab's gentlemanly instincts kick in and he bursts back into life.

'You have come at just the right time, Annie, because we are about to start eating. Can I take your coat?'

'Yes, thank you.' I shrug off my coat, but I can't quite shrug off the awkward atmosphere between us.

'You look very beautiful,' Fab says.

I smooth down the silver sequins on my dress. 'Thanks. I feel like a fish covered in scales.'

Fab laughs. 'A *piekna* fish.'

Just then, the music is stopped and a man in a tight suit steps up to the microphone.

'That's my uncle, Julia's father,' says Fab.

Julia's dad pats his suit down over his ample stomach then says something in Polish.

'It's a toast for the bride and groom,' explains Fab. 'Come on. You're sitting with me.'

He leads me to our table and, sure enough, there is a card with *Annie Demos* written on it in curly lettering. I sit down, but all of a sudden, everyone is standing up again so I jump to my feet.

'*Na zdrowie!*' says the bride's father.

'*Na zdrowie!*' everyone replies, raising their glasses.

Then a chant breaks out: '*Gorzko, gorzko!*'

'What does that mean?' I say to Fab.

He nods towards the bride and groom, who are sitting on a special table at the top of the barn. Julia looks almost unrecognisable from the girl I met at the barbecue. She's wearing a stiff white dress and a veil that's pinned to a complicated, twisty hairstyle. Her smile is the same though. She looks happy. Simon looks happy too, and a little overwhelmed.

'It means "bitter",' Fab says. 'They're saying the vodka is bitter and the bride and groom need to sweeten it with a kiss.'

Bowing under the pressure, Julia and Simon kiss each other, and for some reason everyone counts to ten before applause erupts around the hall.

I look away. All their kissing is reminding me of last night, and I really don't want to think of that right now.

Suddenly, bowls of noodles and vegetables are placed in front of us. Soup is ladled on to the bowls, but Fab waves the waiter away before he can touch mine. He reaches under the table and pulls out a Thermos flask.

'Here,' he says, pouring soup on to my noodles. 'This one hasn't got chicken in it.'

I look at the swirling golden soup. 'Did you make this for me?'

'There are a few vegetarians here and they are having tomato soup, but I wanted you to try real Polish food.'

'Thank you,' I say, still gazing at my steaming bowl.

I've just realised the trouble I must have caused when I rang up this morning. Not only has Fab arranged special food for me, but he would have had to get in touch with Julia and Simon and get the seating plans changed just because I had a sudden whim to see Fab.

I look up at him as he's taking a sip of his soup. His eyes are closed for a second and I can see where he must have nicked himself shaving. The spoon looks too small in his hands.

I see these things in a rush. And other things too, things that I've known but not acknowledged. That at some point before the barbecue in the woods, Fab went there and measured the exact distance from the car park to the blackberry bushes. I think about how he collects the cups for Peggy because he found out that she has arthritis, and how every day this week, before his game of beloved table football, he's played chess with briefcase boy. And that, unlike me, he's bothered to find out briefcase boy's name. It's Adam.

Fab might be the best person I know. Suddenly, I'm filled with certainty that being here with Fab is where I'm supposed to be. *This* is the adventure I've been looking for.

Fab looks up. 'What? Don't you like the soup?'

'I *love* the soup,' I say, then I just smile at Fab, and my smile goes on for so long that he starts to look alarmed.

'Annie, are you feeling OK?'

I nod. 'I feel amazing.' Then I raise my glass and say the first Polish word that pops into my head: '*Gorzko!*'

A man sitting opposite me repeats the word, then everyone around us picks it up, '*Gorzko*, GORZKO!', and soon the whole room is joining in.

Over on the head table, Julia and Simon dutifully put down their soup spoons and kiss.

'I did that,' I say. 'I made two people kiss on command for ten whole seconds!'

'*Na zdrowie!*' says Fab, chinking his glass against mine.

THIRTY-FIVE

The next few hours pass in a blur of potatoes (chips, mash, boiled), stews, salads, fish and vodka shots – or in my case, apple-juice shots. After some pretty serious animal-eating has taken place, the dancing starts up again, presumably to shake things down so that everyone has room for dessert. There is so much dancing and pudding-eating going on that I really don't have the chance to talk to Fab, which is good, because I haven't got a clue what I'm going to say.

At midnight, everyone gathers on the dance floor for the *oczepiny*. I don't know what an *oczepiny* is, but it seems to be something to do with the bride throwing her veil over her shoulder followed by a game that involves passing rolling pins between legs, men running round with women on their backs and balloons being squashed between chests. It's all too much for me so I just watch, and at some point Fab drops out and appears by my side, all red and breathless.

'I need to cool down,' he says. 'Do you want to go for a walk?'

'OK,' I say.

Fab grabs his jacket and we weave our way through the dancing guests and out of the barn doors.

'There is a bench where you can see the river,' says Fab, taking my hand like it's the most natural thing in the world and leading me across the dark lawn. 'Earlier I saw a kingfisher.'

'A kingfisher,' I repeat stupidly.

My heart has sped up, partly because my hand is being held – although that's not making me want to scream, not one tiny bit – but mainly because surely this is it: the moment I've been waiting for.

We sit on a damp bench, Fab lets go of my hand and we both stare in silence at the river. Music drifts across from the barn and I shiver.

Fab says, 'You are quiet tonight.'

'I know,' I say.

Then I take a deep breath of cold air and breathe out slowly. I've never done this before – told someone I've liked them. It's such a little thing, just saying a few words, but for me it's a huge thing.

'There's something I want to tell you,' I say, still staring at the river. 'You know that time in the canteen, after we went blackberry-picking, when I said that I didn't want to go out with anyone?'

Fab laughs. 'As it happens, I do remember that.'

I turn to face him. 'The thing is, Fab, I think I was wrong when I said those things. I mean, I still don't think I want to be anyone's girlfriend, but I do want to be your … something.'

'My something?' He smiles, then shakes his head. 'I don't think you mean that. It is just that I am here, you are here … it's a wedding –'

'But I do mean it!' I don't know what I thought Fab would say, but I expected something more than this. I guess I hoped he'd be pleased, not amused. 'Like I said on the phone, I've missed you.'

He shifts around on the bench and nods. Then he says, 'OK.'

But I know from the look on his face that it's not a *Let's go for it!* OK. It's more of a *This is awkward* OK.

I start to get a horrible feeling inside. 'What's wrong?'

He shrugs. 'It's just, I've seen all the pictures on Instagram.'

I feel cold. Inside and out. 'Instagram? I left my phone

at Oli's party last night. I don't know what you're talking about.'

'The pictures of the party,' he says, and I feel sick because I know exactly what he's going to say next. 'The pictures are of you and your friend, Jim.'

In the excitement of getting ready for the wedding and seeing Fab, I'd almost forgotten about last night. I sigh and shut my eyes for a moment, but there's no use pretending the pictures don't exist.

I hold out my hand. 'I suppose I'd better see them,' I say.

Fab passes me his phone and I find the pictures buried in a load from the party. They were taken by the girl from my English language class, Francesca. There's one of my face mashed into Jim's, our hands all over each other, and the next one shows his hand squeezing my leg and my hands buried in that stupid sheepskin coat he was wearing. I'm smiling in the next one, my eyes closed and my hand resting on Jim's face.

It looks like I'm massively into him, but I know that while those photos were being taken I was thinking about Fab! Everything makes sense now: Fab's strange reaction to me on the phone this morning, the awkward atmosphere when I turned up, how he just looked at me like I was mad when I said I wanted to be his 'something'.

I turn the phone over. I can't stand looking at the pictures any more.

'I didn't know about these,' is all I can think to say.

Fab nudges me. 'Forget about it. Everyone at college will forget about it too. All the time there's stuff going up like this.'

'Pictures that will exist forever.'

'So, ask her to take them down.'

'That won't help if people have already seen them.'

I breathe in the cold air and keep my eyes fixed on the river. My heart is pounding and my legs are shaking. Those pictures tell a story, but one that isn't true, and they make me look like a liar.

I hand his phone back. 'These photos. They're not what they look like. Me and Jim, we were mucking around.'

'Annie, it is not important. Like you keep telling me: we're just friends. You can do what you like. I can do what I like ...' His words seem so cold, so unlike anything I've ever heard Fab say, that I have to turn and look at him.

'*But ... ?*' I say.

'But we are obviously completely different people. I would not kiss someone to "muck around".' He pauses here to draw little speech marks in the air. It's not something I've ever seen him do before. He laughs and shakes

210

his head. 'I would kiss them because I wanted to be their "something"!'

'Well, maybe we are different people,' I say. 'You want a girlfriend, but I don't want a boyfriend. You'd never have a stupid kiss at a party, but it turns out I would. Does it matter if we're different? You said we were perfect together!'

'I think, maybe, that you are not the person I thought you were.'

Fab's not saying this to be mean – he's saying this because it's what he thinks, and this hurts me more than he could imagine. Anger flares up inside me.

'So these photos have totally changed your opinion about me?'

Fab stares straight ahead and keeps his mouth closed. It's like he's shut down and taken away all that warmth that usually flows between us. I want to tell him that if it wasn't for that kiss, I wouldn't be here now, that it made me realise how much I like him, but I can't do that.

'It was a *kiss*, Fab, that's all. You and me, we weren't going out. I haven't cheated on you!'

He nods. 'I know. But that is how it felt when I saw the pictures.'

Suddenly, I have the horrible thought that I might cry. Tonight has been ruined because now I know that from

211

the moment I turned up, Fab has been watching me and judging me.

'I want to go home,' I say.

'You don't have to go home. We are friends, remember?' He says this politely. He says it like he doesn't mean it. 'They haven't even cut the cake yet.'

I turn to look at him. 'I don't think we are friends.'

Still staring at the river, he nods and says, 'Maybe you are right.'

I'm shivering all over and Fab's fists are clenched together. Neither of us can look at each other.

Like I said, everything is ruined.

'Please will you call a taxi for me?' I ask.

'Of course.' He pulls out his phone and dials the number.

After a quick conversation, he tells me that the taxi will take half an hour. We sit in silence. I'm feeling too angry and hurt to speak, and I know Fab is too. I wonder how we're going to fill the time, because I don't think I can stand another minute of this.

'Annie! Fab!' Paulina's voice rings across the lawn. 'Simon and Julia are dancing and it's really funny because Simon can't dance. You've got to come and watch!'

Perfect. I give Fab back his jacket as we walk towards the barn.

'I will find your coat,' he says.

'Thank you.'

Neither of us is using their normal voice. In fact, I feel like I'm walking next to a stranger. And the saddest thing is, I know this is what Fab is feeling too.

THIRTY-SIX

The next morning, I refuse to get out of bed. I just lie there, feeling sad and then feeling annoyed that I kissed Jim, and then angry with Francesca for taking the photos, and then furious with Fab for judging me so quickly. Dark thoughts swirl round my head in a constant cycle until I can't think straight.

As it happens, no one's trying to make me get out of bed, but if they were, I would definitely refuse.

At around eleven o'clock, Mum brings me a cup of tea, but I pretend to be asleep. At twelve she comes into the room all dressed up and tells me she's meeting a friend for a posh roast, whatever that is, and asks if I want to come.

'No,' I mutter, from my cocoon of duvet, pillow and snuggle blanket. I'm now reading *Wuthering Heights* and I've decided that as I've still not got my phone I'm going

214

to lie low for the day and not even go on Facebook. Right now I want to smash up every computer and phone in the world. Well, maybe I'll save one so I don't lose my pictures of Alice and Mabel.

'Are you sure you're OK, Annie?' she asks, glancing at the time on her phone. 'Nothing happened last night?'

I look up at her. 'No. It was fun. I'm just tired.'

'Everything went OK with you and Fab?' she asks, narrowing her eyes.

'Yeah, fine,' I say breezily. *Except that now there is no me and Fab.*

She won't let it go. 'So are you two going out?'

I interrupt her. 'Mum, no one "goes out" these days. We'll just see what happens.'

Mum gets the message and after tucking my hair behind my ear and giving me a lingering worried look that I can't stand, she leaves me alone.

When she gets back, I've fallen asleep and when I wake up I can smell rock buns. Mum makes the best rock buns in the world, but today the smell of butter, sugar and cinnamon does nothing for me.

I plod downstairs with my snuggle blanket wrapped round me and Alice and Mabel balanced on my shoulders. 'Do you want to watch a film?' says Mum. 'It's definitely a film-in-the-afternoon weather.'

'OK,' I say, 'but I only want to watch *Kill Bill*.'

'The one about the woman in a yellow tracksuit hunting down her husband? But I hate that film, Annie. It's so cold and violent.'

I wander into the front room, my snuggle blanket trailing behind me. 'Well, it's the only film I want to watch.'

THIRTY-SEVEN

The next day, I make my way into college rather sheepishly.

I'm hoping that during the course of Sunday, everyone will have conveniently forgotten about the photos of me and Jim, but I realise this isn't going to happen the moment Jackson sits opposite me on the train.

He shakes his head and starts laughing and pretty much keeps this up until we get to our station. Oh, and he also does a bit of tutting and says things like: 'Doesn't the iPhone Six take *detailed* photos?' and 'Did you hear that Jim's been taken to hospital suffering from some sort of animal attack?'

Jackson only shuts up when I threaten to text Amelia and tell her about the time he ate dog food.

I run into Jim as soon as I get to college.

'Dude,' he says, laughing. 'How about those photos?'

I shake my head. 'I know … It seemed like a good idea at the time, right?'

'Yeah, but once me and Mal busked outside Superdrug – we only knew one song, "Wonderwall", and we wore shirts and ties – and that seemed like a good idea at the time too.'

'But did anyone take a series of photos of you doing it then share them with the world?'

'Just my mum, and she only shared them with Mal's mum.' Suddenly, he grins. 'But it was a good party, wasn't it? And as I always say, never regret something that makes you smile!'

I'm fairly certain he never says that.

'I have to admit, I'm experiencing a touch of regret,' I say, glancing around for Fab. I don't want him to turn up and see me sharing a nostalgic post-kiss moment with Jim.

'Are you saying you regret kissing me? Am I a bad kisser?' Jim laughs as he says this, and I'm struck by how different Jim and Fab are. Jim is so easy-going it's like Friday night never happened. There is no weird atmosphere between us, no awkwardness, no pressure. Right now, Jim's almost horizontal approach to life is just what I need.

'I'd give you eight out of ten for your kissing, and that's high … But it did get me into trouble.'

'How come?'

'Oh … it's nothing really. Just that I went to a wedding with Fab on Saturday and he'd seen the photos and he got all angry and jealous about them.'

As soon as the words are out of my mouth, I feel a rush of guilt because I know I shouldn't be talking about Saturday night with Jim, but, for some reason, I don't stop.

'He saw the pictures and wasn't impressed. Said it made him realise what different people we are.' As my mouth runs away from me and I paint Fab as some sort of possessive male, I feel better inside – like it was all for the best – so I twist what happened a bit more. 'I'm obviously the horrible sort of girl who'd get off with someone for a laugh, but Fab would never dream of behaving so disgustingly.'

Jim's face lights up. 'Hey, I'm "the other man". We're in a love triangle!'

I shake my head. 'No, we're not. I'm not in any sort of shape with anyone.'

'What about a cone? That's kind of one-sided.'

'Perfect. I'm in a cone!' I force myself to smile and make my voice as light as his. 'I've got to go and get my phone off Oliver. Oh, and I need to find that Francesca and kick her butt.'

'Tell her she's a perv from me!'

'Will do,' I say.

Then Jim slips his headphones on and we go off in different directions, and I keep my smile fixed in place all the way down the corridor.

THIRTY-EIGHT

rancesca agrees to take the pictures down straight away. She tries to give me some BS about thinking they're 'awesome shots' – she does A-level photography and obviously sees herself as an artist – but I tell her they're just tacky shots and that they violate my human rights. I say all this with a smile on my face so I only scare her a little bit.

After this, I dash across college and grab Oliver before he goes into maths.

'Mum found it down the back of the sofa,' he says, handing over my phone, 'so I told her it belonged to my secret girlfriend.' He sighs woefully. 'But then she found two capes and an eye mask. I probably should have just told her about the party.'

Because of all the business I have to attend to, I get to psychology late. This means I have to stay after the lesson to hand in an essay and then I get to English late. Which I really didn't want to happen.

I push open the door, and everyone turns to look at me.

'Come in, Annie,' says Miss Caudle with a nice smile on her face. She's probably the only person in the room who hasn't seen the pictures of me and Jim. 'Sit down.'

Fab is already at our table so I walk across the room, ignoring the smiles and curious looks being shot in my direction.

Romilly isn't smiling. She's looking a bit heartbroken.

'*I didn't cheat on him!*' I feel like shouting, but, wisely, I just keep my head held high and take my seat next to Fab.

He smiles briefly at me with closed lips and I smile briefly at him with closed lips. I can't quite bring myself to make eye contact with him. Then I get out my books and open my laptop.

'As I was explaining,' says Miss Caudle, 'today we're going to be looking more closely at chapter nine, where Catherine announces her intention of marrying Linton and says it would "degrade" her to marry Heathcliff. Brokenhearted, Heathcliff leaves Wuthering Heights and doesn't return for three years.'

And so begins a very awkward lesson.

Miss Caudle asks us to analyse Catherine's behaviour.

It's fair to say that Fab and I have different interpretations of it.

'Catherine is shallow and thoughtless,' Fab announces with a sigh, leaning back in his chair. 'She decides to marry Linton because he is cheerful, handsome and rich.'

'She's not being thoughtless – she's actually being very thoughtful and practical,' I say. 'She knows that if she marries Linton she can escape the dreary house she lives in and her drunk, violent brother.'

'So, for her own comfort, she breaks the heart of her best friend?'

'Maybe her best friend should see it from her point of view,' I say.

'Maybe *she* should be a bit kinder!' Fab ends this sentence by banging down his pen.

'I think I'm going to answer the questions on my own,' I say.

'Good idea,' mutters Fab, then he turns away from me and starts furiously scribbling notes.

I turn away from him too, and start tapping on my laptop. My chest is aching – in fact, everything inside me seems to be aching – but, slowly, *Wuthering Heights* works its magic on me and I calm down enough to glance over at Fab.

Annoyingly, he's wearing his most normal outfit ever:

dark jeans and a slim-fitting navy shirt. I could have really done with some board shorts or espadrilles today. Fab looks up, like he can sense I'm watching him, and I look back at my work, but not before I notice how being angry seems to have made his eyes a slightly darker shade of blue.

In the course of an average lesson, Fab and I touch each other at least three times, and I've come to expect our brief moments of contact. There's the Hand Brush that happens when one of us borrows a pen or highlighter, then there's the Nudge. Fab nudges me to ask me what words mean, and I nudge him back to tell him to stop interrupting me. Finally, at the end of the lesson, Fab gives me the Shoulder Squeeze. He's so tall that as we leave the room and walk down the corridor, his arm naturally falls across my shoulders.

But not today.

When we get to the classroom door, Fab steps back to let me through, just like he always does, but once we're out in the corridor, he says, 'Goodbye,' and turns and walks in the other direction. He doesn't say it angrily, but he says it like I'm just like any other student in the class.

'Yeah ... Bye,' I say, making sure my voice is just as nonchalant as his, then I rush off to the canteen.

I need a waffle. No, I need *two* waffles, a coffee and a long chat with Hilary.

THIRTY-NINE

'**W**hat an absolute *balls-up*!' says Hilary, which is about as close as she gets to swearing. She clutches her face with horror. 'What a *disaster*!'

'Hilary.' I pull her hands down. 'It's not a disaster – it's a disaster avoided. I mean, obviously I hate us being mean to each other, and the photos are a serious pain in the ass, but overall I'm seeing this as a lucky escape.' I pick up my waffle and stuff a quarter of it into my mouth. I chew for a moment, then add, 'I mean, how could I be with Fab if he expects me never to have kissed another person? I don't know what I was thinking. I'm just relieved that it didn't come to anything.' I sit back in my chair and smile at her. 'See? I'm free as a bird!'

'You don't look free as a bird.'

'Really? What do I look like?'

'Sad.'

I shake my head. '*Tired.*'

'But I thought you, quote, *wanted him more than anything*, unquote?'

'*Shhh!* I wanted a leopard-print body-con dress once, but when it arrived from ASOS I realised I was wrong about that too. Sometimes reality doesn't live up to your expectations.'

'Like Hogwarts?' she says. 'I was so disappointed when I saw the films.'

'Yes, although, strictly speaking, a film isn't reality.'

Hilary's eyes widen as if I've just told her something amazing. Hilary studies further maths, physics, psychology and French, plus Chinese GCSE 'for fun'. She's majorly clever. And yet sometimes she says the silliest things. It's one of the many reasons I love her.

'Here come the boys,' she says, nodding towards the door. I look up and see Jim, Mal and Oliver walking towards us. 'Is this going to be weird? Tell me quickly. I need to know what to do with my face.'

'Not at all weird. I spoke to Jim this morning and he acted like nothing had happened.'

Hilary splutters into her paper coffee cup.

'I know. That reaction itself is pretty weird.'

'Jim's one chilled-out dude.'

'Don't tell him that,' I say. 'It's exactly what he wants to hear.'

Jim drops down on to the sofa next to us, and Oliver and Mal sit on the edge of the table.

'What's up?' says Jim, opening his Dr Pepper, then looking from me to Hilary.

'We were just talking about you and Annie kissing at the party,' she says. 'How funny was that?'

Oliver and Mal's mouths drop open and Jim starts laughing.

'Hilary,' I say, 'you are so full of surprises.'

'Thanks!' she says brightly. 'But it was the funniest thing that happened that night, and *a lot* of funny things happened.'

'Like when Oliver smoked rabbit droppings,' says Mal.

'You put them in the cigarette!' protests Oliver.

Mal ignores him and carries on. 'And when Oliver followed that girl around and kept swooshing his cape around her.'

'I was in character!'

'As a seriously creepy person.'

'I've thought of another funny thing that happened,' says Hilary, and she actually puts her hand up so everyone knows it's her turn to speak. 'Remember when Oliver thought he could fly and jumped off the kitchen table?'

As everyone laughs, Oliver shakes his head. 'This is so unfair,' he says. 'There are only two people here who we should be laughing at.' He looks pointedly at me and then Jim.

'Yeah,' says Jim, 'but me and Annie didn't do a dance where we stroked our own arms.'

'I was referencing an iconic moment from the original *Batman* TV series – season one, nineteen sixty-six! You're all too ignorant to appreciate it.'

Oliver's words make us burst out laughing.

I flop back on to the sofa, unaware that Jim has his arm stretched out behind me. Essentially, I'm laughing my head off in Jim's arms.

And that's when Fab walks by with a plate of presumably discounted crusts.

Our eyes meet for a second, then he turns away, walks over to Adam and sits down with him.

I feel a rush of sadness, which is bizarre because Mal's doing a very accurate impression of Oliver's arm-stroking dance and I really should be laughing.

'Fab looks a bit like Batman today,' Hilary whispers in my ear. 'You know, the good-looking one who freaked out and shouted at that man who walked in on his shot.'

'*Shhh*,' I say, putting my finger to her lips. 'You're not

helping … But, yes, with that top on he does look a bit like Christian Bale.'

'But Fab would *never* speak to someone as rudely as that,' adds Hilary.

'Never,' I'm forced to admit.

FORTY

For the next few days, Fab continues to be perfectly polite, if very frosty, with me. He stops texting me, touching me and talking to me, unless he has to. He even starts agreeing with me in English.

Good, I tell myself, and because I'm still hurt that he could give up on me so quickly, I respond in exactly the same way, with nods and small smiles and definitely no banter or bickering.

But this doesn't stop me missing him.

It begins on Friday.

Miss Caudle tells us our homework is researching Gothic fiction and that we can work alone or in pairs.

Fab says, 'I'm going to make a film.'

I hear the 'I' and respond, 'That takes too long. I'm going to make a poster.' Then I have to watch as he wanders off to find someone else to work with.

I'd have loved to make that film.

Then, at the weekend, I'm reading *Wuthering Heights* and one of the characters says, 'Honest people don't hide their deeds.'

I think, *Fab would like that*, and I reach for my phone so I can text him, but then I remember we don't share quotes any more.

I miss him for quite a long time then. Maybe an hour.

I miss him on Monday when I see him high-five Adam in the corridor and say, 'What's up, my brother?'

I miss him on Wednesday when I notice Jim's wearing a T-shirt that says, *Ironic T-shirt message* and Fab's wearing one that says, *I ♥ Poland*.

And I really miss him on Thursday when I see him pick up a crisp wrapper off the floor and drop it in the bin.

On Friday, I'm hanging around outside sociology, when I look out of the window and see Fab walking across the field. I spot him immediately because he's so tall and because he's the only boy at college still wearing shorts and flip-flops. Like me, he's all on his own. But then Romilly runs up behind him and slips her arm through his. She beams up at him and Fab smiles down at her and they walk into college and out of sight.

Seeing this doesn't make me miss him. It makes me feel like my heart's being squeezed in a vice.

I lean my forehead on the cold glass of the window, staring at the now-empty field, and I try to work out just what's going on in my head. Am I feeling so bad because I'm a jealous person who can't handle Fab talking to another girl? Or am I feeling bad because I've let the best person in my life slip away from me?

'Annie.'

I spin round and see Fab standing in front of me.

'I have a thank-you card for you, from Julia.' He passes me a white envelope.

'Oh … right.' I stare at it in my hands, then look back up at him.

For a moment, we don't say anything, we just stand there as people push past us.

'Well … Have a good weekend,' Fab says, then he walks down the corridor.

'You too,' I say, but I don't think he hears me.

I open the envelope and pull out a card.

Dear Annie,

Thank you for the Playmobil bride and groom. I think they might be our favourite present. Simon superglued them to our bedposts so now we will

232

always remember our special day (and which side of the bed we sleep on!). I hope you like the photo. My cousin is a happy guy, but you take him to the next level!

Buziaczki (kisses)!

Julia

I look in the envelope and see a Polaroid photo. It's of me and Fab and we're sitting at the long table, facing each other and laughing. I didn't even know it had been taken. Fab doesn't look like he's judging me. He looks like he's loving being with me.

How have we come so far from this?

Suddenly, the heart-squeezing starts again, and a bit of nausea is added to it, and then I feel them. Tears, building up in my eyes and threatening to spill down my cheeks. I turn and blink furiously and try to swallow away my sadness. I tell myself that I don't want to go out with Fab. That this would suffocate me. That he's just too old-fashioned and he judged me on the basis of one kiss.

I tell myself that going out with Fab would make me utterly unhappy.

But if that's all true, then how come in this photo I've never looked happier in my life?

FORTY-ONE

I suppress my sadness all the way through sociology and during the train journey home.

Jackson is an excellent distraction, as usual, and tells me a long and rambling story about how Amelia's dad came home from work and caught Jackson sitting on the sofa in his boxer shorts.

'It wasn't rude,' he protests. 'I just can't watch TV in jeans. I get too hot. Plus we were watching the *Simpsons* episode where Bart and Lisa rescue puppies from Mr Burns and I was really laughing so I was hotter than usual.'

'So what happened?' I ask. 'Did he chase you out of the house?'

'No, this is the good bit.' He leans forward, excited to be getting to the punchline. 'Turns out Amelia's dad watches TV in his boxer shorts too! So he took his jeans off and watched *The Simpsons* with us. He said it was great finally being able to relax around me!'

'Jackson, that is such a beautiful story.'

'Thanks, mate.' He sits back and sighs. 'Sad ending though. When her mum came in she said we were both disgusting and were never allowed to do it again, but Trevor – that's Amelia's dad – he gave me this big wink, so I think we will.'

'Dream big,' I say.

When we get to the ticket barrier, I see Mum waiting for me. Just the sight of her smiling little face and floral Marks and Spencer bomber jacket is enough to bring all my sadness back to me. Jackson is so easy to fool, but Mum's a human lie detector.

'See you on Monday,' I say to Jackson, 'and keep your trousers on.'

'Will do,' he says, saluting me.

I turn to face Mum.

'Hi,' I say.

She frowns. 'What's wrong with you?'

And that's all it takes to make my bottom lip start to tremble. I can't talk. If I talk, I cry.

Mum's smile vanishes and she grabs my shoulders. 'What's happened, Annie?' She sounds terrified, and I know why. I *never* cry. Enduring operations, daily pain and almost daily discrimination has toughened me up. I didn't even cry when my nanna died, which I know makes me sound like a massive bitch, but it's just what happened.

'It's Fab,' I finally say. 'He doesn't like me any more!' And because I can't believe those pathetic words have just poured out of my mouth, I burst into tears.

Mum looks baffled – this was not what she expected. Her mouth falls open and her confused face makes me laugh at the same time as crying, but then she strokes my cheek, and I drop the laughing and just go with crying.

'There's only one thing to do in this situation,' she says.

'Go to Pizza Express?' I say, looking up. I love Pizza Express: the dough balls, the cheesecake, the teeny cup of coffee that Mum's started letting me have at the end.

Mum nods and gets out her phone. 'But only if I can get a voucher. Otherwise it's the chippy.'

FORTY-TWO

Over a plate of twelve dough balls, Mum gets the whole story out of me. Well, not the whole story, obviously. I spare her some details about the pictures, like the thigh-squeezing and the visible tongues.

Instead I tell her that the night before I went to the wedding, 'I had a silly kiss with a mate, for a laugh', which is almost the truth, and then I explain that the close proximity between the kiss and me telling Fab I liked him made him go off me.

'Wow …' She peers at me over the edge of her wine glass. 'Looking at it from Fab's point of view, I can see that the photos might have ruined the moment a bit.'

'Mum, when the kiss happened, Fab and I weren't going out or anything. I wouldn't have minded if he'd got off with some girl the night before.'

'*Really?*' She looks incredulous.

'Yes, really.' I take sip of water, not quite able to look at her. 'I don't own him.'

'But what if you saw photos of it? Wouldn't you have questioned whether he genuinely cared about you?'

'No,' I say, then – because I'm starting to feel tearful again – I snatch a dough ball off her plate and shove it in my mouth. 'All right, I wouldn't like it. In fact, I'd hate it. I'd think he was a dick. Thanks, Mum. You've made me realise that Fab thinks I'm a massive dick!' I groan and put my head in my hands.

Mum leans forward and gives my shoulder a pat. 'You're not a massive dick, love. You just had a dick-ish moment – a regrettable kiss – and we've all had those.'

'Fab hasn't,' I say.

'Well, if he hasn't yet, he will one day.'

This makes me feel a bit better. 'But what can I do now? We're barely talking to each other!'

Mum shrugs. 'I guess it depends how much you like him.'

'I like him a lot. I wish I didn't, but I do. I think about him all the time and I miss talking to him. I even miss him looking at me!'

'Then think of a way to prove this to him. Sometimes actions speak louder than words … and photos on Instagram.'

'It's going to have to be an action of epic proportions to speak louder than those.'

Around us, plates clatter, children shriek and the chefs call out to each other.

'You're nothing if not determined, Annie,' says Mum. 'I'll tell you something your dad did for me. You know he's scared of heights? Well, he once took me up the Eiffel Tower because he knew that was what I wanted to do more than anything else in the world.'

'Really?' It's not often I hear Mum telling me a story about Dad being nice. He moved out before I was born, then went back to Greece just after I was diagnosed with cerebral palsy. He's told me the two aren't connected, but like Mum said, sometimes actions speak louder than words. 'How did he handle it? Last time he was over he refused to go on the London Eye with me.'

Mum laughs. 'Not well. He was sick – not over the edge, thank God.'

'So, you're saying I need to do the equivalent of making myself vomit for Fab?'

She grins. 'Kind of! Think of what is important to him and give it to him.'

I nod, my mind already running through what's important to Fab.

'Right,' she says, 'it's my turn to talk. I've got some exciting news from school.'

I look up. 'What happened?'

'A fox ran into the playground during playtime and it caused mayhem!'

When we get home, I go up to my room and put on some music. I let Alice and Mabel out of their cage, then pick up *Wuthering Heights*. But the book is only a prop because my mind is just going over and over what Mum said at Pizza Express. What could I do to show Fab just what he means to me? To show that I'm sincere and not the sort of person who only does things on a whim?

My first thought is table football, simply because he loves playing it. Could I practise in secret then blow him away with my skills? No. That's rubbish. It has to be better than that.

I run through Fab's other favourite things: pork ... books ... toast ... helping people ... Actually, what doesn't he like? He loves everything! Whatever I choose, it has to be special to just the two of us.

Alice hops over to me and investigates the pages of *Wuthering Heights*.

'Are you a book sniffer too, Alice?' I say.

She ignores me. Obviously. She's a rat, but even so I add, 'That's Fab's favourite bit.'

I sit up, making Alice jump away.

Wuthering Heights … That's it! The only person I know who loves *Wuthering Heights* as much as I do is Fab. He even told me once – arms waving around – that Emily Brontë's descriptions of the moors were 'majestic' and that one day he would see them with his own eyes. Miss Caudle told us you can visit Haworth, the parsonage where Emily wrote *Wuthering Heights*. Miss said you can even walk to Top Withens, the ruined house that's supposed to be the inspiration for Wuthering Heights.

I push all practical problems to one side – access issues, the journey, money – and just focus on the look on Fab's face when I tell him where we're going. He was excited about blackberry-picking. Top Withens will blow his mind!

'Sorry,' I say, lifting Mabel off my laptop. 'I've got an epic romantic gesture to plan. I'm taking Fab to Wuthering Heights.'

FORTY-THREE

All weekend, I work out how I can get Fab to Haworth, looking into train times, buses and the opening hours of the parsonage. The more the plan takes shape in my mind, the more convinced I become that it's going to work. I tell Mum and she thinks it's a great idea, but that it's too far for us to go on our own. She says I have to wait until she can take us in the car. I point out that not only is she being a very uncool mum, but having her there would make it the worst romantic gesture ever. She just laughs and tells me to think of a romantic gesture that isn't two hundred and fifty miles away and then she'll be a cool mum.

To be honest, we have a bit of an argument about it that ends with her saying: 'Accept it, Annie. You're not going.'

Oh, but I am. Because next weekend Mum's going to

stay with her friend and she believes Hilary and I are having a girly sleepover.

Hilary *is* sleeping over, but only on the Friday night, then on Saturday morning Hilary's going home and I'm whisking Fab off to the Yorkshire moors.

Back at college, it's easy enough to persuade Hilary to lie for me – she'd do anything to see her OTP get together – but she thinks I'm making a mistake keeping it a secret from Fab.

'What if he's not in when you turn up?' she asks.

'It'll be fine,' I say, pushing this thought to the back of my mind, along with an even worse thought: that Fab will be in, but will refuse to go with me.

The trip has become so real in my mind, so vivid, that there are moments when I want to rush across the common room and blurt it all out to Fab, but I don't, because there's still this frosty force field surrounding us. So I keep quiet and tell myself that he won't be able to resist the offer of a trip to Haworth and that at some point on Saturday all the frostiness between us will magically vanish … I don't know exactly when this will happen, but I'm convinced that at some point – between eating sandwiches on the train and buying Brontë fudge in the gift shop – Fab's arm will fall across my shoulders and I'll rest against him, our eyes will meet and – *bam!* – Fannie will burst into life again.

FORTY-FOUR

'You girls have fun,' says Mum, leaning out of the car window. 'There's pizza and ice cream in the freezer and I made a nut roast for Sunday. You can have your very own roast dinner!'

'Yummy!' says Hilary.

Mum starts the engine. 'Look after each other, and promise me: no parties.' She wags her finger as she says this.

'We promise,' I say. Then I nudge Hilary.

'No way,' adds Hilary. 'We definitely won't be having a party.'

'And, Annie ...' Mum fixes me with a look, 'don't you dare go to Haworth.'

'What?' I say, laughing loudly. 'I'm not going anywhere!'

We wave until the car's disappeared around the corner. Then we go inside and shut the door behind us. I rest against it.

'I laughed too hard, didn't I?' I say.

'Just a bit,' says Hilary, grinning at me.

'Now come upstairs and help me choose a running-away-to-Haworth outfit.'

While Hilary sits on my bed, offering opinions on the clothes I'm holding up, Alice and Mabel fight on her lap.

Once we've got my bottom half sorted out – jeans (it's going to be cold), and my favourite white and platinum Nikes – we move on to my top half.

'Do I want a fluffy jumper or a cool sweatshirt with cats on it?'

'What's on the jumper?'

'A pineapple.'

'Wear the sweatshirt because it looks warmer. You're practically going to Scotland. It's going to be freezing.'

'That's it then.' I chuck the cat sweatshirt on top of my jeans. 'I just need to find Bananagrams then I'm ready.' I pile my hair up on my head and twist a band round it.

'What's Bananagrams?'

'A game,' I say. 'We're going to play it on the train.'

'Are you feeling nervous?' asks Hilary.

Nervous doesn't really cover it. I nod, and say, 'A bit.'

'Don't worry.' Hilary lifts Alice and Mabel back into their cage. 'When do romantic gestures in films backfire? Never! Now tell me what you're doing.'

I've already told her several times, but she knows it calms me down to repeat it. 'Tomorrow, at six thirty, we'll get the train together.'

'I'll leave you at the station and you'll get a taxi to Fab's.'

I nod. 'That's it. And I'll say, "Come to Haworth with me!" He says, "Amazing!", jumps in the taxi, then it's back to the station to catch the train to London. Three different trains and a bus later, we're in Haworth. We visit the Brontë parsonage, have a quick walk on the moors and then it's back to Haworth for a cream tea – I know Fab will love cream teas – then we do the same journey home, but in reverse.'

'What could go wrong?' she says.

'Nothing!' I say, making my voice extra bright so that it sounds convincing.

FORTY-FIVE

Getting Hilary up and on the six-thirty train is hard work, but I manage it, and as dawn breaks I'm pulling up outside Fab's house in a taxi. I felt quite calm on the train, with Hilary chatting away about her plans to paint her bedroom, but now my heart's beating as fast as the taxi driver's dance music.

'Will you wait for me?' I say. 'I've just got to get my friend then we're going back to the station.'

'You're the boss,' he says, drumming his fingers on the steering wheel. He keeps the engine running while I walk up the path.

I don't ring the doorbell in case it wakes up Fab's mum. Instead, I find Fab's bedroom window and throw a small stone at it. Ghost Cathy taps on the window in *Wuthering Heights* so I thought this would be the perfect way to start our adventure. The stone misses. So I try another – a bigger one this time.

Fab still doesn't appear.

Aware of the taxi waiting behind me, meter running, music thudding, I pick up a handful of tiny stones and hurl them at the window. They bounce off and fall all over me.

'Ow!' I say.

'*Annie?* What are you doing?'

I look up and see Fab standing in the doorway holding a bowl of cereal. He's barefoot and wearing shorts.

'I thought you'd be asleep,' I whisper.

He frowns at me. 'No. I needed to be up early. Why are you here? Why didn't you ring the doorbell?'

Now I'm face-to-face with Fab, pretending to be a fictitious ghost seems like a pretty silly thing to do. 'I wanted to surprise you.'

His eyes widen. 'Trust me. I am surprised.'

I shake my head. 'No, *this* isn't the surprise.' I walk over to him and look him in the eyes. 'Fab, I've come to take you to Haworth!'

He blinks. 'I do not understand.'

Behind me, the taxi driver beeps his horn, startling me.

'Look,' I say, 'I haven't got time to explain, but you need to grab a coat and put on some jeans because

Haworth is in Yorkshire, and that's up north, and it's cold up there.' Fab continues staring at me like I'm mad, so I add, 'You're always saying that you want to see the moors where *Wuthering Heights* is set, so let's go!'

He shivers and folds his arms. 'Annie, are you joking?'

'*No!* Now hurry up. The train's leaving soon and if we're going to get to Haworth and back in one day we need to get a move on.'

'But I'm helping my uncle Emil build a shed. How long will it take?'

'Fab, it's over two hundred miles away, so it will take a long time, but we'll be back by tonight.'

Slowly he shakes his head, and all my dreams and plans start to slip away from me. This wasn't supposed to happen. Fab was supposed to laugh, throw a coat on and jump in the taxi with me!

'I'm sorry, Annie, but I have to put up the shed and I'm going to Julia's this evening to see her honeymoon pictures. I promised I'd make a cheesecake –'

'*Cheesecake?*' My voice rises. 'Fab, I've spent over one hundred pounds on train tickets. I've planned everything. We're going to walk on the moors. We'll see Emily's dog's collar!'

'Well, you should have told me about your surprise and checked to see if I was free first!'

'But then it wouldn't have been a surprise, would it? I thought you'd find this *exciting*. We're going to have an adventure.'

We stare at each other and for a moment I think he might change his mind, but then that shutdown look comes over his face, the one I've seen so much of in the past two weeks, and he says, 'No. It is impossible.'

'When have you ever said that something is impossible?' I burst out. 'With you, anything is possible: table football, games of rounders, blackberrying trips. Trust me, this trip is very possible.'

He shakes his head. 'Maybe we can go another time. I'm sorry you wasted your money.'

Suddenly, I'm not sure if I actually want to go with Fab. All his energy that I love so much seems to have vanished.

'I haven't wasted my money,' I say, 'because I'm still going!' I turn and walk towards the taxi.

Still holding his cereal, he runs after me in his bare feet. 'You can't go on your own,' he says, grabbing my arm.

I shake him off. 'Oh really? Just watch me!' I get out my wallet and find the train tickets. 'I booked for the ten-past-eight train and I'm going to be on it. Here's your ticket.' I throw it at his chest and it flutters to the floor. Then I yank the taxi door open. Before I get in, I shout, 'Enjoy putting up a shed!'

'I will!' he shouts back.

I slam the door. 'Just drive,' I say to the taxi driver, which is something I've always wanted to say, only I thought it would feel better than this.

We pull away from the kerb and I stare straight ahead, my arms folded. Out of the corner of my eye, I can see Fab watching me. He's scowling and he looks deeply disapproving. I have to clamp my lips shut to stop myself from sticking my tongue out at him.

Once we're back on the main road, the taxi driver says, 'So … Didn't go according to plan?'

'Nope.'

'Just you getting that train now?'

I nod, and keep my eyes on the road ahead.

'Sure you still want to go?'

'Definitely,' I say. I've never been so sure of anything in my life. If it's the last thing I do, I am getting on that train and going to Haworth – and I'll take hundreds of photos and send them to Fab all day so he knows exactly what he's missing!

The driver turns his music up. 'You're the boss!'

FORTY-SIX

Back at the station, I have time to buy a hot chocolate and a cheese croissant before going to the platform.

I sit in my wheelchair and even though it's too hot I take a sip of my drink. Sugar sweeps through my body. This is what I need to calm me down. Behind me, a train comes to a hissing stop. I know that it's heading back towards my town and I'm struck by how easy it would be just to turn round, get on that train and go home.

But how many times have I sat on the train going to college, dreaming that I don't get off and that I keep going? And now I'm on the brink of doing just that. I might have planned on doing this with Fab, but I can still do it on my own.

The train to London arrives with a screech of brakes and a blast of cold air, and as I push myself into the carriage, I see the train on the opposite platform roll out

252

of the station. *I'm actually doing this*, I think, and immediately my stomach squeezes and my heart speeds up.

I transfer to my reserved seat, get out my croissant and start peeling warm, greasy strips off it. My nausea is caused by my hunger, I tell myself, not by worry. But even if I *am* worried, that's fine, isn't it? Didn't I tell Jackson that nausea is the sensation that accompanies all the best, coolest things in life?

Jackson … I'd love to have Jackson with me right now.

The whistle blows, the train starts to move forward and my heart beats even faster. I stare out of the window as we glide past the platform. We pass a woman reading a book, a pigeon attacking a crisp packet, a man checking his watch, then we're going through a tunnel and we're out in the countryside.

A bag lands on the seat next to me with a thud.

Looking up, I see Fab. He's bent over and gasping for breath.

My heart leaps. 'You came!'

His cheeks are red and he's still wearing the shorts and hoodie he had on at his house, but he's put on a pair of trainers and thrown his leather jacket on. Without speaking or even looking at me, he pushes his bag to one side, sits down, gets out a bottle of water and gulps it down. He screws the lid on tight then turns to face me.

'I had to run to the station and it took me seventeen minutes. Three miles in seventeen minutes, Annie! This ...' he pauses here to indicate his cheeks and dishevelled hair, 'is all your fault!'

He looks angry, so I make my face suitably serious even though I want to grin with happiness.

'Thank you,' I say, and he nods and drinks more water. 'Would you like some cheese croissant?'

He shakes his head. 'No, thank you. I don't feel too great. I had to run very fast.'

'Sorry, but I'm glad you decided to come. I promise we're going to have a good time.'

He holds up a finger in front of my face. He hasn't done this to me in ages and just the sight of that pompous finger makes the smile rise up inside me again. The finger wags from side to side. 'I didn't *decide* to come, Annie. You blackmailed me. There is a difference.'

'Well, thank you anyway. You won't regret it.'

'I already do,' he says, leaning forward and resting his face in his hands. 'My mother is angry with me, and when Emil and Julia discover I have gone off, they will feel let down.'

'Maybe they'll feel happy for you,' I risk saying, 'because you're doing an exciting thing with a friend?'

He looks at me out of the corner of his eye. 'Maybe,'

he concedes, 'if they know I'm with you.' Then he pulls out his phone and starts tapping away.

This is not exactly how I pictured the train journey. I thought we'd be chatting, united in shared anticipation of the rest of the day, and possibly playing Bananagrams, but instead Fab's acting like I've kidnapped him and he has the distinct air of a victim. I tell myself that the important thing is that he's sitting next to me. Once he's calmed down, he'll start to enjoy himself, and enjoy being with me.

Tap, tap, tap, he goes on his phone, pausing only to glower out of the window.

I'll definitely save Bananagrams until later.

FORTY-SEVEN

All the way to London, Fab sits hunched over his phone, his leather jacket squeaking, sending an apparently endless series of texts while I read my book. It's only as we're pulling into Victoria station that I risk speaking to him again.

'I'm guessing you were really looking forward to making that cheesecake,' I say.

'I was. The cheesecake was going to be passion-fruit flavour. Yesterday, I cycled eight miles to Aldi to buy the ten passion fruit I needed.'

'Were they cheap?'

He nods and smiles begrudgingly. 'Yes, three for sixty-nine pence.'

It's not much of a conversation, but it's a start, and I just got the first smile I've had from him in days.

Victoria station perks Fab up, and when we're through

the ticket barrier, he looks around, taking in the chaos. His eyes light up when a woman dressed as a giant piece of sushi offers us a free sashimi roll.

'OK,' he says, after he's persuaded her to give him three. 'I have eaten. I feel much better. So what happens next?'

'We cross London. We've got just under an hour until our train goes from King's Cross.'

'So let's go.'

'There's one little problem,' I say, pointing at my wheelchair. 'Victoria Tube station doesn't have a lift.'

'Seriously?'

'They're building the lift shafts as we speak. So we have a choice: we can either get the bus, or I can walk through the Underground while you carry my wheelchair.'

Fab considers the two options. 'If we only have an hour, then I think we should take the Tube, but it will be a lot of walking for you.'

'I'll be fine,' I say. 'Let's go.'

Because of all the folding and unfolding of the wheelchair and one broken-down escalator, we get to King's Cross with only a few minutes to spare. Moments after we've boarded the train, it starts to move.

When we find our seats, I haven't quite got the energy

to get out of my wheelchair. 'I think I'll hang out here for a minute,' I say.

'And I will find the buffet,' says Fab. 'What would you like?'

'Just a sandwich.' I take a ten-pound note out of my wallet.

He shakes his head. 'I can buy this.'

'I know, but I don't want you to. I've planned this whole day out. It's supposed to be a treat for you.'

After a moment's hesitation, he takes the money, then walks down the carriage, swaying with the movement of the train.

For the next few minutes, I sit in my wheelchair and look out of the window, enjoying seeing things I've never seen before in my life. They're not very exciting things – back gardens, graffiti-covered car parks, some wasteland piled high with tyres – but it's all new to me and I don't want to miss a thing.

When Fab gets back, he's carrying a bulging paper bag. 'There was a meal deal,' he says. Then, looking pleased with himself, he arranges crisps, sandwiches and juice on the little table. After he's sat down, he pulls a Twix out of his pocket. 'And this is for you.'

I don't think the shiny golden wrapper has ever looked more beautiful.

I can't quite bring myself to look at him. 'They're my favourite,' I say.

'I know.'

'Thank you.'

'Annie, it's just a Twix,' he says with a shrug, but then he smiles, and it's one of his huge smiles, and I think, maybe, just maybe, this is going to work.

FORTY-EIGHT

The journey might not be exactly like I imagined it – it takes longer for one thing, and there are no games of Bananagrams – but by the time we're on the bus to Haworth, we're more like ourselves again, laughing and teasing each other.

'That's definitely a moor,' I say, tapping the window of the bus.

'No.' Fab shakes his head. 'Moors are big and flat. That is a big field.'

'You wouldn't know. You've never seen a moor in your life.'

'Neither have you,' he says, then we spend the rest of the journey with our eyes glued to the window, because whether it's a moor or a field, we know we're getting close now. Really close.

We're dropped off in a car park on the edge of Haworth

and immediately I'm struck by how cold it is. The temperature seems to have dropped a few degrees even since we left Leeds. Fab zips up his leather jacket and blows on his fingers.

'Ready to admit you're regretting the shorts?' I say, pulling my coat around me. It may be fluffy, but the wind is whipping through it.

'No, because I am not regretting the shorts. I am like Heathcliff: too tough to feel the cold.' Then, to prove his point, he slaps his thighs enthusiastically, making a passing tourist jump. 'I am sorry!' Fab says, putting a comforting hand on her shoulder, making her jump even more.

I look around the car park. 'Well, we're here,' I say.

'We are?'

'Yes, look.' I point at a house that's just peeking through the trees. 'That's it. That's Emily Brontë's home.'

'It is? *Really?*'

I laugh. 'Yes, *really.*'

A smile breaks out on his face. 'We're actually here.'

'Can you believe it?'

He laughs and shakes his head. 'Not really. This morning I was about to make a cheesecake and now I'm looking at Emily Brontë's house.'

'Come on,' I say. 'Let's find that dog collar.'

* * *

261

We buy our tickets and the lady tells us we're lucky, it's quiet today, then I leave my wheelchair with her and we walk through a stone hallway and into the dining room. It's small, with patterned wallpaper, and scattered across a table are pens and ink, paper and manuscripts. We stand behind the security rope.

'It feels like they have just left the room,' says Fab.

'I know.' And even though we are the only ones in the room, for some reason we're lowering our voices, like we're in a church.

'Can you feel it?' he says.

'What?'

'*Wuthering Heights*? This is where it came alive.'

For a moment, I don't do or say anything. I just stand on the edge of the room – so neat, so plain – and I try to imagine something extraordinary coming to life here. A clock ticks and a floorboard creaks. I wonder if Emily heard those sounds as she sat at the table, a pen in her hand.

'I think I can feel it,' I say. 'Just a whisper of it.'

'Me too,' Fab says, and his hand rests on my shoulder for the first time since the wedding.

The house is full of these whispers, ghosts of Emily and *Wuthering Heights*. I feel glimmers of them when I peer into her small, white bedroom, and again when I'm staring at her cracked christening mug. I even feel a little shiver down my spine when we find the shiny copper collar that belonged to Keeper, Emily's dog. We've been joking about this collar, but now we're here, and it's in front of us and it's so solid and real, it seems incredible that Emily Brontë's hands clipped it around Keeper's neck.

We're both quiet as we walk around the house, reading every single label and staring at each object, but it's not like before. It's not a cold, frosty silence. It's comfortable and it's something we're sharing.

When we've looked in all the rooms and wandered around the gift shop, we go outside and discover that sunshine has finally broken through the clouds. We stand next to each other, and look up to the moors.

'Told you they were moors,' I say.

'You were right,' Fab says with a nod.

I hoped coming here would bring us back to life, and it has – almost. Our arms are just touching, and our eyes meet and we smile at each other, but I want more than this.

'You know we can walk to Top Withens,' I say.

'It's too far,' says Fab, without taking his eyes off the hills.

'No, it's not. It's two and a half miles … ish, and we can get a taxi for the first bit, then there's this road – not big enough for a car, but fine for a wheelchair. It's only at the end that I'd need to walk. I can do it easily.' *Well, maybe not easily*, I think.

'But what will you do with your wheelchair?'

'Hide it,' I say with a shrug.

'And you think we have enough time?' He looks doubtful, and this only makes me more determined to go.

'We don't have to get the bus for a couple of hours. It'll be fine.' I can tell Fab is tempted, so I give him a nudge. 'Isn't it what you've always wanted to do? Walk where Heathcliff and Cathy walked? Fab, we can see where they lived!'

He looks at me and smiles. 'We'll turn back if it gets too late.'

FORTY-NINE

It's easy enough to get Haworth's one and only taxi driver, Bob, to pick us up at the parsonage and take us as far as he can go along the track.

'You're not really dressed for a hike,' he says, as he unloads my wheelchair from the boot.

I'm not sure if he's talking about Fab's shorts or my fluffy coat.

'The weather's lovely,' I say, my face raised to the sun. 'We'll be fine.'

'The weather can turn round here,' Bob says darkly, and I share a smile with Fab because the comment is very *Wuthering Heights*-ish.

After agreeing to pick us up when we ring, Bob reverses down the track, and Fab and I set off.

I'm fit. I go to the gym. I lift weights, but still my arms begin to ache after the first mile. What I hadn't realised when I studied Google Maps so obsessively was that the track sloped ever so gently upwards and right now my triceps are burning. Still, my arms may be aching, but I feel strong inside.

The sun is shining down on us and we are just where I hoped we'd be.

I stop to shake out my arms.

'Do you want me to push?' Fab asks.

I shake my head. 'I'm good.'

After a while, the smooth road turns into a gritty track and my wheelchair grinds to a halt. 'This is as far as she goes,' I say, getting to my feet. 'We need a hiding place.'

We look around, peering over the dry-stone wall. When I imagined doing this, I thought there'd be some convenient bushes that I could slide the wheelchair under, but it turns out moors are flat and empty, and totally devoid of any wheelchair-sized hiding places.

'Maybe we should turn back,' says Fab. 'This is fantastic, Annie, but we don't need to go to Top Withens. Look.' He throws his arms out wide. 'We're on the moors. We made it!'

I shake my head. 'We do need to go further. Just a bit. We're so close.'

In the end, we leave the wheelchair behind a wall with

a note stuck to it that says, *Owner has popped out for a walk. Back soon. Don't take!!*

'What sort of scumbag would steal a wheelchair?' I say, as we start walking up the track. 'I mean, there's hardly anyone out here, so what are the chances of a wheelchair thief turning up?'

'Zero,' admits Fab.

Then he offers me his arm and I take it. Still the sun shines on us and I feel this wave of confidence, telling me I was so right to do this. Me and Fab, we're nearly there. I can tell.

We pass the Brontë waterfall, which right now is more of a Brontë puddle, and then start to climb. Far away, we see that clouds are gathering. Fab's eyes flick anxiously from the clouds to me.

'Look,' I say, pointing towards a black silhouette on a distant hill. 'There it is: Top Withens!'

'Wuthering Heights,' says Fab.

'It could be ...'

We stand and stare at the lonely ruin clinging to the side of the hill. Between us and the house is a patchwork of fields – green, bright orange, dark purple. The path we need to take twists through these fields, up higher and higher. We start to walk, and all around us, rust-coloured ferns and grasses sway in the wind.

'It's like we're in the middle of the sea,' I say.

Fab nods, his eyes taking everything in.

I think both of us know that it's getting late, too late, and that it's taking me longer to walk than I thought it would, but now we can see Top Withens, I don't think anything could stop us from getting there. The last stretch is the hardest, and the muscles in my legs hurt so much that I have to concentrate on one step at a time and keep my eyes fixed on our goal.

And then we are there, standing in the crumbling shadow of Wuthering Heights.

I put my hands on the cold, damp wall and Fab instinctively does the same. Then, laughing, I turn and sink to the ground, my back against the wall, my face raised to the last, weak rays of sunshine. I shut my eyes.

'It's too small to be Wuthering Heights,' I say.

'And there isn't a walled courtyard,' calls out Fab, who has disappeared inside the ruin.

But I don't care that this building is nothing like Wuthering Heights, because I am seeing what Emily Brontë saw, and I'm feeling the freedom she felt, and I know why she loved it here.

Fab comes and sits next to me and we eat the Emily chocolate that we bought in the gift shop.

'How strange to have a bar of chocolate named after you.'

'It is good chocolate,' says Fab.

We know we can't stay long. The light is fading, the clouds are getting darker and I've already had to recalculate our train times. If we can get back to Haworth in an hour and a half, then we'll get home just before midnight. I don't tell Fab this.

He's running around taking photos on his phone, exclaiming about the 'stunning sky' and 'immense clouds'. They really are immense. Actually, they're worryingly immense.

'Come on,' I shout. 'We need to go.'

To begin with, it's easier retracing our steps. It's downhill, plus the chocolate has given me energy, but then it begins to rain and the icy drops that hit us are hard and fat.

'Ow,' I say. 'That's painful rain.'

Fab winces. 'It is like needles!'

For the next couple of minutes, we laugh as the rain comes down, claiming we're like Lockwood getting caught in the snow.

'Maybe we should turn back,' I say, 'and shelter at Wuthering Heights.'

'There will be log fires, candles.'

'Porridge,' I add. 'They always have a lot of porridge.'

'I hate porridge, but right now I'd eat ten bowls of it.'

Then the rain gets harder, and soon my fake fur coat is a sad, sodden thing and Fab is shivering. The rain trickles down the back of my neck, into my ears; it even runs down the small of my back and into my pants.

I have rain in my pants. This is a first.

Laughing, we cling on to each other, for warmth and to stop me falling on the slippery stone. I squeeze his arm and he gives me a weak smile.

'The weather does turn quickly round here,' he says, or rather shouts, in my ear.

And then it starts to snow.

I have a brief moment of *Ah … snow!* because it really does look pretty, but Fab seems less impressed. I guess he's used to snow in Poland.

'We need to get down,' he says, trying to make me walk faster. 'We could lose the path if it gets thicker.'

'Relax,' I say through chattering teeth. 'We're only twenty minutes to my wheelchair and five minutes later we'll be in the taxi.'

We plod on in silence, snow settling on our heads and shoulders, back past the waterfall, then on to the track.

'This is it!' I use my last bit of energy to run to the wall where we hid my wheelchair, but when I peer over, I can't see it anywhere. 'Fab,' I shout, 'it's gone!'

270

'You must have the wrong wall.'

'No, I remember we left it opposite the spooky skeleton tree.' I point at the tree next to us. 'There it is: spooky skeleton tree. We put it here!'

Fab searches up and down the rest of the wall, and I look again where I know we left it, and that's when I see the sodden piece of paper, half covered in snow.

'Look.' I hold up the note, my voice rising in panic. 'Someone's actually stolen my wheelchair!'

He examines the note, his face buried in the collar of his leather jacket, snow covering his hair. 'So we ring for the taxi. Maybe he can get further along the track this time.'

'Fab, you're not listening to me. My wheelchair has *gone*. It cost hundreds of pounds!'

He brushes snow off his face. 'And we are stuck on the moors in a storm. Possibly lost, because I wasn't paying attention when the taxi drove us up here. We can worry about your wheelchair later.' He pulls his phone out and tries to shield it from the snow. 'No reception. You try.'

'Nothing,' I say, pointlessly waving my phone around in the air. 'I had reception when we were dropped off.'

'So let's go,' says Fab, then he sticks out his arm, waiting for me to link arms with him.

'I'm fine,' I say, because I'm annoyed, and not just

271

because Mum is going to kill me for losing my wheelchair.

I'm annoyed because I've lost my wheelchair for no reason. Yes, we made it to Haworth – we even got to Top Withens – but I thought at some point Fab would reach out to me somehow, but he hasn't. It's almost like we've been on a school trip, minus the teachers and other students, and I've spent the day hanging out with a good friend. We'll get back to Haworth, go home, and then what? We'll just carry on being good friends? I wanted so much more than that!

And now we're not even acting like friends. Fab's bossing me around and yelling.

'You should wear my jacket,' he says when he catches up with me, making it sound like an order.

We stumble forward, heads bent over.

'Why?' I say. 'There's no reason why I should be dry and you should get soaked.'

'There's no reason, Annie. I am saying it to be *kind*. And maybe if you are a bit warmer, you would walk faster and then we would have a chance of working out where we are, getting off this moor and getting home tonight!'

'Great. Thanks for making me feel bad *again*.'

Fab makes a sound of annoyance and we plod on. The

snow is falling in fatter clumps now and we're pushing through it with our feet.

After several seconds, Fab asks, 'What do you mean? *Make you feel bad again?* When have I ever made you feel bad?'

I stop walking. 'Have you forgotten what happened at the wedding? The kiss?'

He turns to face me. 'Why do you have to bring that up?'

'Because from the way you've been acting since – hardly speaking to me, never touching me – it's obvious that it still massively bothers you. I brought you here to prove to you what you mean to me, hoping you'd realise that that kiss meant nothing to me, but it didn't work, did it? Because you, Fabian Kaczka, are just too proud to forgive me!' I shout these last words out loudly, and we stand there, staring at each other, the snow swirling around us.

I seriously want to stomp off and bang a door, and I'm fairly certain Fab wants to do something similar because he's breathing very heavily and his fists are screwed up. But we can't do that because we're trapped on a moor. In fact, I don't think I can take another step, and if we're ever going to get home, I think I'm going to have to do the opposite of storming off.

'Can I have a piggyback?' I snap.

'Yes, you can!' he snaps back. Then he turns round and crouches down.

I climb up on to his shoulders and he lifts me up in the air. For a few minutes, I cling on in silent fury, like a pissed-off baby koala. This is so infantilising ... But at least I have easy access to his ear.

'I'm not enjoying this,' I say. 'In fact, I'm *hating* this.'

'So am I. You are as heavy as a pile of bricks.'

'Yeah? Well, you're no pixie, Fab. You're like an actual giant!'

'It is a good job I am an actual giant, or I wouldn't be able to carry you out of this mess *you* got us into!'

This makes me growl with rage, which in turn makes Fab shake me. Yes. He is actually shaking me from side to side! So I squeeze him with my knees and arms, and then he jogs extra bouncily.

Snow falls all around us. My face is numb with cold. I stop squeezing and rest against his back, and Fab stops jogging. In fact, he stops walking altogether.

We just stand like this. I can feel my heart thudding into his back and his hair damp against my cheek.

'Annie, I have been speaking to you,' he says, 'and I have been touching you.' To prove this, he gives my legs a squeeze. 'See? I even came all the way to Haworth with you. What else do you want?'

Snow sticks to my eyelashes, my shoulders and my fingers. It settles on Fab's face.

After a moment, I say, 'I wanted you to kiss me.' A gust of wind makes the snow swirl into us. 'I wanted to bring you to a place we both love and I wanted you to understand what that meant and I wanted you to kiss me. But it was a stupid idea.'

I know from our English lessons that Fab goes quiet when he thinks. Right now he is absolutely silent. Then he says, 'It was not a stupid idea. It was a beautiful idea.'

I rest my icy cheek against his, and he reaches up and puts his hand on my wet hair, and that's how we're standing when the beam of a torch falls on our faces, and Bob appears, flat cap pulled low on his head.

'Stop canoodling, you bloody idiots,' he says, 'and follow me. Cab's this way.'

Then he turns and trudges back the way he came, and we follow him.

FIFTY

We're so wet that Bob insists we sit on his dog's blanket, then he reverses down the narrow, bumpy track. Fab and I shiver in the back of the cab, fluffy dog hair sticking to our soaking clothes. My hands are shaking so much that it takes several attempts to do up my seat belt.

'Feeling the cold?' I manage to say.

'A little,' admits Fab, leaning against me for warmth.

'I was considering sending out a search party,' Bob says, eyeing us in the rear-view mirror.

'Someone took my wheelchair,' I say, and I feel tears welling up in my eyes.

He chuckles. '*I* took your wheelchair. I came looking for you and spotted it. Well, I didn't want to leave it in the snow getting all rusty so I popped it in the boot. Then I got my flashlight out and started searching for you.'

I look at Fab and laugh, relief rushing through me and warming me up slightly.

'We need a lift to Keighley,' I say, working out how much money I've got left. 'If we're going to make it home tonight we need to get the six-twenty train.'

Bob chuckles again. He seems to be enjoying this. 'There are no trains going out of Keighley. They're all cancelled because of the snow. It's frost heave that does it. Moves the tracks.'

I turn to Fab. 'What are we going to do?'

Fab leans forward. 'Bob, is there a youth hostel near here?'

'We've got a lovely youth hostel. That's the best idea. You two need to warm up.'

I let my head fall against Fab's shoulder.

'We'll go home tomorrow,' says Fab. 'It'll be fine.'

'But there might not be any room in the hostel and we don't know what it costs and –'

'So, now you've got your adventure.'

I laugh through chattering teeth. 'I really have, haven't I?'

FIFTY-ONE

The youth hostel is incredible, a Gothic mansion set on the edge of Haworth, surrounded by trees.

As Bob unloads my wheelchair from the boot, I ask Fab, 'Are we actually allowed to stay here?'

'Of course,' says Fab. 'We are youth! Come on.'

Inside, he starts chatting to the man behind the reception desk. Fab's obviously much better at handling the cold because while he's stopped shivering in the taxi, my teeth are still chattering and my fingers are white. We're lucky: the disabled-access room is available and we're even allowed to rummage through the lost property for dry clothes. Which is how I end up curled up on a bottom bunk in a huge pair of tracksuit bottoms, odd hiking socks and a slightly sweaty rugby shirt.

Fab disappears to get changed and, more importantly, to make us a cup of tea. I pull the lime-green duvet over me. The radiator's cranked up as high as it will go, and slowly, slowly, I feel myself begin to thaw out and my aching body loses its numbness.

Once my fingers are working, I ring Mum and tell her some rubbish about Hilary and me having a great time making cupcakes and watching old movies. She's very giggly so I'm guessing her and Amanda have hit the Prosecco, which is good because hopefully she'll forget all about me and won't try and ring later on the landline.

Fab backs into the room holding two mugs.

'Wow,' I say. 'That is a tight T-shirt.'

'Yes, I think it might be a lady's, but at least it is dry.'

I sit up and he passes me my tea.

'This place is amazing, Annie. There is a kitchen with a cupboard full of forgotten food so I am cooking pasta and a Hungarian boy has given me some sauce – vegetarian – and there are games and films.'

I wrap my hands round my mug, take a sip and close my eyes.

'Good?' he asks.

'Pure bliss … And, look: I've stopped shaking.'

When Fab goes to check on the pasta, I finish my tea, then lie back on the bed and send Hilary a message: **Staying the night in Haworth. Long story. It involves snow.**

Romantic! is her reply.

Well, I have to put her straight. No, cold. And right now I'm wearing a sweaty stranger's rugby shirt.

Super romantic!! I get back.

FIFTY-TWO

Fab's pasta might be the best I've ever eaten, but then everything I experience at the youth hostel that evening is the very best: the shower, the game of Scrabble, the Hungarian biscuits that Edvin shares with us, the overwashed smoothness of my lime-green duvet cover.

By some unspoken agreement, Fab and I avoid the whole 'I wanted you to kiss me' situation in the snow. In fact, we're almost walking on eggshells around each other, being exceptionally polite and gentle.

When it's time to go to bed, Fab tactfully disappears for five minutes then knocks on the door and asks, 'Can I come in?' It's like we've entered our very own version of a Victorian novel.

We lie in the dark on our bunk beds and I tell Fab that tonight has had a rosy glow around it.

'Even the water in the shower felt softer than at home,' I say to the bottom of his bunk. 'Did you notice?'

'It's because you got so extremely cold and tired.' His deep voice drifts down to me. 'Anything that follows that has to be good.'

'Maybe that's why people swim in icy water or climb mountains. Just so they can experience a mind-blowing cup of tea afterwards.'

'Maybe.'

We fall quiet and after a while I wonder if Fab's fallen asleep. I hope he hasn't because there's something I want to tell him.

I push at the bottom of his mattress. 'Hey, Fab. Are you awake?'

I hear him turn over. 'Yes.'

'I want to tell you a story.'

'Really? I am very sleepy.'

'You can go to sleep if you want. I'll just talk.'

After a moment, he says, 'OK. Tell me your story.'

'So, it's about a little girl, a little girl who would only wear boys' clothes and who had a lot of curly hair that she routinely cut off herself, despite her mum hiding all the scissors.'

'Just to be clear, is the little girl's name Annie?'

'It might be.' I turn over my pillow so that my face is

lying on the cool side. Somewhere across the room the radiator ticks. 'One day, when this girl was six, she was doing an Easter bonnet parade at her school and she noticed that people were staring at her, and the strangest thing was that they weren't staring at the excellent plastic dinosaurs she'd stuck all over her bonnet – they were staring at her walk. *How strange*, she thought to herself. *Why would anyone be interested in my walk? Haven't they seen the ceratosaurus I stuck right in the middle of my hat?* But they really were staring at her walk, because it wasn't normal, and normal – the girl soon discovered – was *the* aim of life … You still awake up there?'

'Still awake,' Fab says. 'This is a very interesting story.'

'Isn't it? We haven't even got to the good bit yet. The little girl soon realised that when people are determined to tell you that there is something wrong with you, then you have a choice: you can either give in and believe them, or fight them. So she fought. When a friend described maths as "retarded", she told them not to use that word. When a teacher said she was brave for auditioning for the lead role of Annie in the school play, she asked, "Why is it brave?" And when people stared, she stared right back.'

'That does sound quite brave,' Fab says.

'Not brave. Necessary … and often tiring.'

Fab doesn't speak, but I know he's listening.

'Fast-forward a few years, and the little girl has become exactly the same age as me. She has fought to be seen as a valuable human being and, as a result, she's as tough as a limpet's tooth. Do you know why she's as tough as a limpet's tooth?'

'No. I do not even know what a limpet is.'

'It's a tiny, shelled sea creature that clings to rocks.'

He goes quiet for a moment. 'Is she as tough as a limpet's tooth because a limpet's tooth is very strong?'

'Yes! In fact, it's the strongest material on earth.'

'I thought that was a diamond.'

'A common misconception. This girl is so tough that all the comments and stares and pity just bounce off her. Which is great. Except she's become so good at protecting herself that sometimes the good stuff bounces off too.'

'That's not so good.' Fab sounds wide awake.

'No, although it's never really been a problem until she meets a giant.'

'A Polish giant?'

'Yes!'

'He sounds incredible and extremely handsome.'

'He is,' I say. Then, into the silence of the room, I add, 'You are.'

284

It feels as though Fab and I are hovering on the brink, holding our breath.

Fab doesn't speak, so I carry on. 'The giant calls the girl *moja dziewczyna*, and this scares her because she has spent so long getting the world to see her for who she is.'

'And who is she?'

'She's not "the disabled girl". She's not anyone's girl. She's Annie.'

The bunk squeaks and Fab's arm reaches over the side of the bunk. He wiggles his fingers.

'And I'm not a giant. I'm Fab.'

After a moment, I slip my hand into his. Our fingers entwine and I feel a lightness drift through my whole body.

'I often feel scared too,' he says.

'You do?'

'Yes, but about different things. I don't know where my home is. My mother and father …' he pauses as he tries to find the right words, 'I feel like I must look after them, but I can't look after both of them. I am pulled between two different places and two different people. But then I met you, and I felt certain about something.' His hand is warm in mine. I don't want to let go. 'It felt like coming home.'

'I like that story,' I say.

'I liked yours. But it didn't have an ending?'

I hold his hand tighter. 'I don't know how it ends.'

Get down off your bunk, I think with all my might, willing the message to spread from my mind, up through my hand, my fingers and into Fab. *Come and see me!* More than anything, I want to wrap my arms around him and hold him tight. I was freezing earlier – even my bones felt cold – but now my whole body is glowing.

But I know he won't. Because Fab Kaczka is such a bloody gentleman.

FIFTY-THREE

When I wake up the next morning, the room is strangely bright and Fab's hand is still dangling over the edge of the bunk.

'Hey,' I say, giving it a tug. 'Are you awake?'

His fingers tighten round mine for a second, then he lets go and the bunk shakes as he sits up. 'What time is it?'

I find my phone. 'It's *ten*. We've slept for hours!'

I sit on the edge of my bed, then, wincing, I pull on my jeans. Every muscle in my body hurts. Slowly, I go to the window and pull back the curtain.

'Snow!' I say.

It was dark when we arrived so we couldn't see anything out of the window, but it turns out our room is facing the moors, and they are covered in thick, deep, perfect snow. I press my fingers on the cold glass.

'Fab, you've got to come and look.'

He joins me at the window.

'Have you ever seen snow sparkle like this? It looks like a fairytale!'

'It looks like it will stop buses,' he replies.

I groan and, while Fab starts throwing things in his bag, I ring the bus company. Fab's right: all the buses out of Haworth have been cancelled.

I hang up. 'Fab, I need to get back. My mum's coming home at six and she'll be mad with me if she finds out I came here. She specifically said: "Annie, don't you dare go to Haworth!"'

'We will get back in time.'

'But how? There are no buses and Bob "the only taxi driver in Haworth" told us he doesn't work Sundays. After I've paid for the youth hostel, I've got less than twenty pounds and I don't even think that will be enough for a taxi from Keighley. We're trapped in Haworth!'

'Unfortunately, I only have ten pounds,' he says, peering into his wallet, 'but there is always a solution.'

Even though I'm worried, I can't help smiling, because it's so good to have invincible Fab back again, even if it is a wildly optimistic, invincible Fab.

He gives me one of his biggest smiles. 'I will go and get

us some breakfast and at the same time find us a way out of here.'

Ten minutes later, I'm eating toast in the back of Edvin's Ford Fiesta. Fab's up front with Edvin, who's taking us to a service station, where Fab is confident he can convince a Polish lorry driver to give us a lift closer to home.

I lean forward. 'You really think this will work?'

'Of course it will work,' Fab says, then he rummages through Edvin's CD collection and holds up an album by someone called Yanni. '*Sensuous Chill*,' Fab reads. 'Annie, this is what you need to listen to right now.'

Fab's plan does work, and at the service station we swap Yanni for a prog rock singer called Agnieszka Świta and the Ford Fiesta for a thirty-six-tonne articulated lorry.

Our new driver is called Milek, and as we pull out on to the motorway he tells us that he can't talk as he needs to concentrate. 'Driving a lorry like this is a huge responsibility,' he says – at least, that's what Fab tells me because Milek doesn't speak English so Fab's translating for me.

The good news is that Milek is on his way back to Poland and can drop us at a service station very close to home. The bad news is it's going to take four hours to get there. I do a quick calculation and realise that I can still make it home before Mum.

'*Nie zatrzyma,*' Milek says as he shifts through the gears.

'What's that?' I ask Fab.

'We don't stop.'

'What? Not at all?'

Fab shrugs. 'Apparently not.'

Feeling relieved that I went to the toilet at the service station, I ball my damp coat into a pillow and lean against the window.

As we travel along the motorway, the snow-covered fields gradually fade away and by the time we hit the Midlands, it's hard to believe we dug a car out of snow this morning. Next to me, Fab alternates between singing along to Agnieszka Świta and talking to Milek in Polish – although Milek doesn't talk much, he doesn't seem to mind if Fab talks. Polish sounds so relaxing – like water tumbling over stones – that it's hard to stay awake.

When we finally pull into the service station, my back's aching, I'm dying for a wee and I've listened to the same Agnieszka Świta album five times. Milek really needs to expand his music collection.

Inside, Fab goes into the cafe to buy Milek a coffee, while I head to the toilets. When I come out, I find Fab sitting at a table by the window. He's texting and in front of him are three steaming drinks. I sit opposite him, sip my coffee and look out of the window. I watch the constant flow of cars in and out of the car park. It's grey outside and already starting to get dark. Rain trickles down the glass.

I smile, then see my reflection smile. This is what my big romantic gesture has come down to: a sticky table in a service station, 'Wrecking Ball' blaring out of some speakers courtesy of UK Services FM and the powerful smell of fried egg.

Milek appears for his coffee. We say thank you, and just before he goes, he nods at me then says something to Fab in Polish.

Fab shrugs, and says, '*Może.*'

'You were talking about me, weren't you?' I ask when he's gone.

Fab laughs. 'Yes.'

'So tell me. What did he say?'

Fab wraps his hands round his mug. 'He asked me if you were my girl.'

I sit up, suddenly feeling more awake. 'Oh ... And what did you say?'

For a moment, Fab doesn't say anything. He just looks at me. So I look right back at him, meeting his gaze.

'I told him that although I don't call you "my girl" as such, that is what you feel like to me, because when I am

291

with you, life is better. In fact, I told him *I* am better when I'm with you.'

'Really?' I manage to say. 'You said all that with just one word?'

He nods. 'Yes, Polish is very economical. But that is not all. I also told him that I will never try to change you or take anything away from you, that you will never be *my* anything. You are Annie: the girl who gave me *Wuthering Heights*.'

My heart beats faster and a woman brushes past me with a tray. All I can say is: 'But you said I wasn't the person you thought I was.'

Fab doesn't take his eyes off me. 'You're not, and that's why this has been the most wonderful adventure.'

Around us, people talk, cups bang down, knives and forks scrape across plates. But for me, the world is standing still.

'So.' He reaches across the table and takes my hands in his. 'You and me, Annie and Fab, are we *a thing*?'

I take a deep breath. 'If you'd like to be my thing, then I'd like to be your thing.'

He squeezes my fingers. 'I would like to be your thing.'

And at that moment, at that *exact* moment, 'Blurred Lines' fades out and UK Services FM decide the travellers of Great Britain need to hear Kate Bush sing 'Wuthering Heights'.

My eyes widen. 'Fab, have you heard what they're playing?'

'It's the song that isn't our song,' he says.

'Don't I owe you a dance?'

'Really?' Fab glances round the cafe. 'You think we should dance *right* here?'

'Maybe over there.' I nod towards the entrance. 'Between the toilets and the slot machines.'

He laughs. 'But I thought you hated slow dancing?'

'Who says it's going to be slow? Come on, life's too short for embarrassment, Fab.'

'You're right!'

He takes my hand and together we weave between the tables and chairs. When we get to the fruit machine, he bows and says, 'Annie, will you dance with me?'

'It would be my pleasure,' I say, stepping into his arms as the music builds up.

Fab pulls me close and he moves me around the small space, past a man in a football shirt and between the racks of discounted DVDs. We shuffle round in circles, just like those couples at Sophie's party. I rest my head on Fab's chest and he rests his hand on my back. The end of the song is cut off abruptly by a traffic report about a hold-up on the M40. By now, we're back by the slot machines, arms wrapped around each other, our hearts beating together. Behind us, the machines buzz and ping.

Fab puts one hand on the back of my head, and I reach up on my toes and I pull him towards me, my slightly damp fur coat pressing into his leather jacket, and our lips meet for a kiss. A kiss that is so familiar, so exciting, so utterly right, that it really feels like coming home and the start of something, all at the same time.

FIFTY-FOUR

When Mum's car pulls up outside the house, I'm curled up on the sofa reading *Wuthering Heights*.

'Hello, love!' she shouts as she opens the front door.

'I'm in here,' I call from the front room, then I watch her in the hallway as she drops her bag on the floor, shrugs off her coat and unwinds her scarf. 'Was it fun?'

She bends down and pulls off her boots. 'Brilliant, but I'm knackered. I don't know how I'm going to go to work tomorrow.'

I lean my head back and let my aching body melt into the sofa. About seven minutes ago, a lorry loaded with fruit and with *Cytrusy!* written on the sides dropped me off outside my house. About six minutes ago, I waved goodbye to Fab, and he shouted, '*Żegnaj, piękna dziewczyna!*' out of the window. He shouted it so loud, he made our next-door neighbour's cat shoot across the road.

Mum comes in and flops next to me on the sofa. 'So,' she says, turning to face me, 'how was your weekend?'

'Oh, you know … Quiet,' I say, then I smile. And the smile gets bigger and bigger until it's out of control and spreading across my face and taking on Cheshire cat proportions. Too late, I try to hide my huge smile behind *Wuthering Heights*.

Mum gasps. '*You went*, didn't you?'

'I don't know what you're talking about, Mother.'

She snatches the book away. 'Don't even try to lie to me, Annie Demos. Did you, or did you not go to Haworth with Fab?'

I decide it's impossible to fight the smile and I let it run free. 'Yes!' I say, throwing my arms wide. 'And I don't care what you do to me!'

FIFTY-FIVE

So what does being someone's thing look like?

Actually, it doesn't *look* very different to not being someone's thing. I still get the train every day with Jackson and recently we've given the cows names. We're considering taking a trip to visit them, but we're worried they won't recognise us. I spend break with Hilary and the boys, eating waffles and talking nonsense. Sometimes Fab joins us, but only for a bit. He's got too much energy and too many friends to stay in one place for long, even if I'm in that place.

We've moved on from *Wuthering Heights* in English. Now we're reading Joseph Conrad's *Heart of Darkness*. Fab loves it. I hate it. Miss Caudle says that our arguments are resulting in the best essays she's ever marked.

Fab's made me passion-fruit cheesecake and he's met Alice and Mabel. He passed the test.

We've been on two dates, and both involved members of Fab's family so on Saturday we're going on one of our own, to Pizza Express. Mum's got us a voucher. Fab's never eaten a dough ball before so I've decided to overcome my fear of overtly romantic situations so I can introduce him to one of my favourite food items.

I am Annie. He is Fab.

This is our story, and we don't have a clue how it ends.

ACKNOWLEDGEMENTS

I would like to thank my wonderful editor, Zoe Griffiths, for her excellent advice, and Hannah Sandford whose early insights helped so much. I feel lucky to be published by Bloomsbury and to have worked with such a fantastic group of people.

Thank you to Agnieszka Oliwa, who patiently helped me with the Polish words and phrases and described Polish weddings so temptingly. If there are any mistakes, they are my own!

I am hugely grateful to my agent, Julia Churchill, and for the support I get from the team at A.M. Heath. Julia offers the wisest council; her belief in my writing means a great deal to me.

Finally, I would like to extend a very special thanks to my first readers, Lauren Huggett and Chloe Smith, whose advice, support and suggestions have been invaluable. Thank you, Lauren and Chloe, for helping me to tell Annie's story.

Sometimes life needs a little bit of chaos...

When Meg looks at the
stars, she sees adventure.
She sees escape. She sees
her future. Because
Meg's big ambition is to
become an astronaut.

But her hopes are
thrown into chaos
when her mum
disappears to follow up yet another of her
Very Important Causes … and leaves Meg and her
baby sister behind.

Can Meg take care of Elsa and still follow her own
path? She'll need a miracle of cosmic proportions. But
then nobody ever got anywhere by dreaming small …

Sometimes life needs a little bit of chaos

STARGAZING FOR BEGINNERS

JENNY McLACHLAN

TURN OVER FOR A SNEAK PEEK

ONE

On my seventh birthday, Grandad made me a rocket. He used the cardboard box the washing machine came in, put a cone on the top and painted the whole thing white. Then he stencilled *MEGARA 1* on the side with red paint.

Mum took her hands away from my eyes and I blinked. The rocket nearly touched the ceiling. 'Is it real?' I asked.

'Almost,' she said.

Grandad handed me my bike helmet. 'Are you ready for your first mission, Meg?'

I nodded. 'I think so.'

I was already wearing my astronaut pyjamas so all I had to do was put on the helmet and climb inside the rocket. Mum handed me a broken keyboard – my control panel – then shut the door. I ran my hands over the keys. Grandad had stuck labels on the different buttons: fuel boost, disengage, pressure drop. One button was painted green and simply said, *LIFT-OFF*.

'Megara 1,' Grandad said, putting on his smoothest American accent, 'you're good at one minute.'

'Roger,' I replied. Grandad and I were always watching NASA documentaries so I knew exactly what to say.

'Megara 1, this is Houston. You are go for staging.'

'Inboard cut off,' I said, tapping buttons randomly, 'staging and ignition.' At that exact moment a deep growl burst out and I realised Mum had turned on the vacuum cleaner. Its roar filled the cardboard rocket. I felt my heart speed up with excitement and I tightened my grip on the keyboard.

'Megara 1, this is Houston!' Grandad shouted to be heard over the vac. 'Thrust is GO. All engines. You're looking good. This is ten seconds and counting.'

'Ten,' I called out, 'nine … eight …'

Grandad and Mum joined in. 'Seven … six … five …' Then one of them started shaking the rocket around.

'Mum!'

'What is it?' Her face appeared at the cut-out window.

'I'm scared!'

She reached through the window and took hold of my hand. Her silver rings pressed into my skin. 'Don't be scared, Meg. I'm here.'

'Four ... three ... two ... one ...' continued Grandad.

'All engines running,' I said, then I slammed my finger down on the green button. 'Launch commit!'

'Lift-off!' shouted Grandad. 'We have lift-off!'

Mum let go of my hand and disappeared.

The vac roared, the rocket shook wildly from side to side and I was leaving Earth and shooting into deepest space!

TWO

Eight years later. Back on planet Earth.

Before I get my breakfast, I make sure everything in my bedroom is just right.

I smooth down the duvet, push the chair under the desk and turn my globe so England is facing the sun. Then I get a red pen and cross yesterday off my homework timetable. Good. If I spend a couple of hours working on my speech tonight then I'll be right on track. I don't believe in luck or superstition, but before I leave the room I take a moment to glance at my picture of Valentina Tereshkova – the first woman to fly in space. Her steely gaze keeps me focused during the day.

I grab some Weetabix from the kitchen then follow the *thud, thud, thud* coming from the front room. Only

Mum would play bass anthems at eight in the morning. I find her kneeling on the floor, blowing up a paddling pool. Sitting on the sofa is my sister, Elsa, a jammy crust dangling out of her mouth.

I turn down the music then join Elsa. I start eating my cereal, trying to ignore Elsa's powerful wee smell. Her nappy looks suspiciously bulgy.

There's a hiss of air as Mum pushes in a plastic stopper. 'Looking forward to trying out our new paddling pool?'

'Not really,' I say. 'Mum, we live in a flat. Why do we need a paddling pool?'

'So we can have *fun*, Meg! I thought we could fill it up and pretend summer's here.'

I look around. Toys, clothes and books are spread all over the carpet and Pongo is running round and round the paddling pool, barking at the inflated rings. 'Mum, there isn't enough room for it in here.'

'There's loads of room,' she says, then she jumps to her feet. 'I'm going to start filling it up.'

Elsa takes the crust out of her mouth and holds it out to me.

'No thanks,' I say, but she keeps jabbing it in my direction.

'Da!' she says. 'Da, da!'

'OK, OK.' I take it off her and pretend to eat it. 'Nom, nom,' I say. 'Happy now?'

Elsa smiles, sticks her thumb in her mouth and flops back on the sofa. Then we watch as Mum runs to and from the kitchen with pans of steaming water. She's wearing her Tinker Bell nightie and her bleached-blonde dreads are gathered on the top of her head with a scrunchie. Her bracelets jangle as each pan of water splashes into the pool.

After six trips, the water just about covers the bottom. 'It's going to take ages,' she says sadly, swishing a toe in the water. 'Can you help me, Meg?'

'Sorry. I've got to get to school.' I go to the mirror over the mantelpiece and start brushing my hair back into a ponytail.

'Such beautiful hair,' says Mum. I can see her in the mirror watching me, her turquoise nose stud gleaming on her pale face. We look so different: me with my dark eyes and hair and Mum, blue-eyed and with hair so blonde it's almost white. 'I wish you'd wear it down.'

'It's easier this way.' I smooth a strand of hair behind my ear and button up my blazer. I brush some toast crumbs off my shoulder. 'Shouldn't you be getting ready for work, Mum?'

'In a minute. I'll just put a bit more water in.'

Mum runs the Mencap charity shop in town. That's her paid job, but she's got loads of others, like fundraising for Greenpeace and running the community allotment. She wants to make the planet a cleaner, better place. It's fair to say she doesn't feel the same way about our flat.

'Meg, can you babysit Elsa after school?' Mum dumps another pan of water into the paddling pool. 'You know my friend Sara, the nurse?' I shake my head. Mum's got so many friends I can't keep up with them all. 'Well, Sara's going to do some volunteer work abroad and she needs a lift to the airport.'

'I don't know ...' I think about tonight's jam-packed square on my homework timetable. 'I've got so much work to do ... Plus I've got to practise my speech.'

Mum looks at me, eyes wide. 'I'll be back around six. You and Elsa can just hang out together until then. It'll be fun!'

I look at Elsa, who's now lying on her back on the sofa, gurgling and trying to get her foot in her mouth. 'You really need to give Sara a lift?'

'It would help her out a lot,' Mum says, then she pulls me into a hug, pressing my face into her hair and I smell the sandalwood incense she loves so much.

I put up with it for a moment then wriggle out of her arms. 'OK,' I say.

Mum's face lights up. 'What would I do without you?'

Over Mum's shoulder, I see Elsa crawl towards the edge of the sofa, reaching for Pongo's tail. *'Mum!'* I say, but already Elsa is losing her balance. She wobbles for a second then tumbles forward, landing on the floor with a thud.

There's this moment of silence before the screaming starts. Mum darts across the room and scoops Elsa up. 'Poor baby!' she says, showering her with kisses. Pongo jumps up and tries to stick his pointy nose between them.

'I'm going now,' I say, but they don't hear me. Now Pongo's been pulled into the hug too and his excited barks rise over Elsa's screams. I slip out of the flat and shut the door behind me.

Immediately, I'm hit by the quiet, the bright cold air and the view.

Our flat might be small and damp, but it's got the best view in town. I stand on the balcony and look from the houses of the estate to my school. Beyond school, I see the hotels, the sea and the pier. Then I look up at the sky, higher and higher, until I find the moon. It's a white smudge that's disappearing fast.

I turn and run down the concrete stairway, my feet ringing out with each step.

I've got to get to school. I've got so much to do.

THREE

School's good. I get one hundred per cent in a maths test, finally learn how to conjugate German verbs and spend lunchtime in the library researching my favourite star, Alpha Centauri B.

When I know the canteen will be quiet, I go and get some lunch. It looks like almost everyone's been chucked out, but some students from my year – Bella Lofthouse and her friends – are still sitting round a table while the lunchtime supervisors clean up. As I walk past, they glance over at me, and I see Bella's lips curve up in a smile. Quickly, I turn away. Bella is always laughing with her friends and she finds me particularly funny. The longer I hang around the more likely it is that she'll say something to me and somehow I'll end up looking stupid. I grab the first sandwich I see – egg mayonnaise – pay for it, then walk straight out of the canteen.

It's at times like this that I miss Harriet. She was my best friend at school. OK, she was my only friend in or out of school, but that didn't matter because we were soul mates, and we did everything together – walking to school, eating lunch, talking for hours on the phone, sleepovers … Harriet even went camping with me and Mum every summer. Then, one day, she told me that her mum and dad were talking about moving to New Zealand. Five months later, she was gone.

When a huge star dies, there is a massive explosion, a supernova, and later, all that's left is a dark, dense black hole where no light can get in or out. From brilliant lightness to total darkness: that's what it felt like when Harriet left.

When I got over the shock of her going and looked around me, there didn't seem to be a place for me anywhere: everyone else was paired up or in groups. I did try to talk to people, wriggle into their conversations, but Harriet had always done the talking for both of us and I was out of practice. Plus, like I said, I was shocked when she went and feeling a bit like a dark, dense black hole.

Who wants to be friends with a dark, dense black hole? No one!

All that darkness has gone now, but the friend-making

moment seems to have passed by. Which is why, right now, I'm leaning against the wall by the girls' toilets eating an egg sandwich all on my own.

Like I said. Sometimes I miss Harriet.

FALL IN LOVE
WiTH THE WARMTH, WiT, ROMANCE AND FiERCE FRIENDSHIPS OF BEA, BETTY, KAT AND PEARL'S LiVES IN

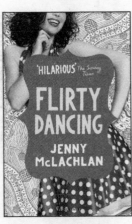

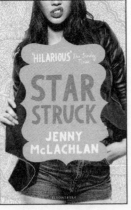